VOODOO

KRISTINE ALLEN

VOODOO, 1st Edition Copyright 2020 by Kristine Allen, Demented Sons Publishing.
All Rights Reserved.
ISBN-13: 9798646991851

Published in the United States of America. First published in June, 2020.

Cover Design: Jay Aheer, Simply Defined Art
Photographer: Eric McKinney, Cover'd by 6:12 www.612photog.com
Cover Model: Gus Smyrnios
Editing: Olivia Ventura and Ginny Gaylor, Hot Tree Editing, www.hottreeediting.com
Formatting: Champagne Book Design, www.champagnebookdesign.com

The purchase of this e-book, or book, allows you one legal copy for your own personal reading enjoyment on your personal computer or device. This does not include the right to resell, distribute, print or transfer this book, in whole or in part to anyone, in any format, via methods either currently known or yet to be invented, or upload to a file sharing peer to peer program, except in the case of brief quotations embodied in critical reviews and certain other noncommercial uses. It may not be re-sold or given away to other people. Such action is illegal and in violation of the U.S. Copyright Law. Criminal copyright infringement, including infringement without monetary gain, is investigated by the FBI and is punishable by up to 5 years in federal prison and a fine of $250,000 (http://www.fbi.gov/ipr/). Thank you for respecting the hard work of this author.

This is a work of fiction. Names, characters, businesses, places, events, and incidents are either the product of the author's imagination or used in a fictitious manner. Any resemblance to actual persons, living or dead, or actual events is purely coincidental. The publisher does not have any control and does not assume any responsibility for author or third-party websites or their content. For information, contact the author at kristine.allen.author@gmail.com. Thank you for supporting this author and her rights.

Warning: This dark romance book contains offensive language, violence and sexual situations. Mature audiences only, 18+ years of age.

To Ms. Sherman. I don't know where you are now, or if your name is still the same, but you're the reason I'm addicted to reading. Thank you for holding me enthralled as you read to us in your third grade class in Okinawa, Japan. I'm sorry my taste in books got a little dirty and twisted over the years.

ROYAL BASTARDS MC

Where loyalty is king!
27 Authors. 26 Stories. One Hell of a ride!
Visit us here: royalbastardsmc.com

The books in this series are standalones and can be read in any order.

Bonus Holiday Releases:

Crimson Syn—**A Biker for Christmas**
Nikki Landis—**The Biker's Gift**
Glenna Maynard—**The Biker's Kiss**

2020 Release Schedule for the **Royal Bastards MC:**

Erin Trejo Jan 7th
Chelle C. Craze * Eli Abbot Jan 14th
K Webster Jan 21st
Esther E. Schmidt Jan 28th
Elizabeth Knox Feb 4th
Glenna Maynard Feb 11th
Madison Faye Feb 18th
CM Genovese Feb 25th
J. Lynn Lombard Mar 3rd
Crimson Syn Mar 10th
B.B. Blaque Mar 17th
Addison Jane Mar 24th
Izzy Sweet & Sean Moriarty Mar 31st
Nikki Landis Apr 7th
KL Ramsey Apr 14th
M. Merin Apr 21st
Sapphire Knight Apr 28th
Bink Cummings May 5th
Winter Travers May 12th
Linny Lawless May 19th
Jax Hart May 26th
Kristine Allen Jun 2nd
Elle Boon Jun 9th
Ker Dukey Jun 16th
KE Osborn Jun 23rd
Shannon Youngblood June 30th

Special thanks to **Crimson Syn, Nikki Landis, Sean Moriarty, Izzy Sweet, Shannon Youngblood, Khloe Wren, Teagan Brooks, M. Merin,** and **Elizabeth Knox** who loaned me characters from their books or who have characters mentioned in Voodoo.

Crimson, thank you for being my sounding board through this book. Nikki, thank you for helping me spread my paranormal wings. I'm dang near giddy about this book's release! Thank you for all your hard work in the RBMC organization. It's appreciated more than you know. Y'all have been amazing and I'm so glad to call you friends after this project. Bring on round two!

Sean and Izzy, I love y'all to pieces. I'm stealing you and claiming you as my friends after this whether you like it or not. After all the FBI worthy discussions we've had, we can't be anything less. Izzy, thanks for being a good sport about the unicorn ornament. LOL.

Teagan, I know you aren't in this round, but you're awesome and I'm so glad we've become friends. The next signing we have together will involve alcohol and lots of it. You truly are my soul sister.

Kristin, thank you for being the best damn PA a girl could ask for as well as keeping this rowdy bunch of authors in line! I'm so glad you love Voodoo. It makes my heart happy.

I'm Ogun "Voodoo" Dupré—Enforcer for the Ankeny RBMC. There's no pretty way to put it, I do the dirty work for my club. Without question, I follow the direct orders of my president.

Except when my services were required for a particularly delicate situation, I found myself hesitating for the first time in my adult life. That hesitation was my downfall.

With the *Bratva* gunning for me and my own father out for my blood, I didn't think I'd survive. Yet, come hell or high water, I'd keep her safe—because she was meant to be mine.

The rumors about my chapter are true, yet things aren't always what they seem. We don't play fair, and we don't leave witnesses.

Sometimes you gotta work a little black magic to come out alive.

ROYAL BASTARDS CODE

PROTECT: The club and your brothers come before anything else and must be protected at all costs. CLUB is FAMILY.

RESPECT: Earn it & Give it. Respect club law. Respect the patch. Respect your brothers. Disrespect a member and there will be hell to pay.

HONOR: Being patched in is an honor, not a right. Your colors are sacred, not to be left alone, and NEVER let them touch the ground.

OL' LADIES: Never disrespect a member's or brother's ol' lady. PERIOD.

CHURCH is MANDATORY.

LOYALTY: Takes precedence over all, including well-being.

HONESTY: Never LIE, CHEAT, or STEAL from another member or the club.

TERRITORY: You are to respect your brothers' property and follow their Chapter's club rules.

TRUST: Years to earn it… seconds to lose it.

NEVER RIDE OFF: Brothers do not abandon their family.

PROLOGUE

The average person walking around in society today lives in a self-imposed bubble of ignorance. Like if they pretend their little reality is all sunshine and roses, the darkness of the world doesn't exist close to them. They choose to ignore the necessary evil that exists around them every single day. Close enough to touch. In their backyard. Maybe even in their own bed.

My first initiation into evil was when I was younger than most. Then again, I was born with a piece of it in me. Simmering deep under the surface. Though my grandmother had taught me to control it, there was no eradicating it. So I'd learned to embrace it when the need arose and bury it when it wasn't necessary.

Sometimes I buried it in alcohol, sometimes drugs, other times, women. When those things weren't available, I kept it tightly leashed. Gnashing its teeth, straining at its tethers, and burning relentlessly.

I'm Ogun "Voodoo" Dupré, and this is my story.

Six Years Old…

"Ogun, get your backpack, baby. Hurry. Granmè is waiting for us." My mama was rushing me, and I was dragging my feet. I was hungry. I wanted a snack before we left.

"Mama, I want a snack." I pouted as my shoulders hunched.

"Not now." She glanced over her shoulder to the front door. The rumble of Papa's bike was coming down the road. The ever-present blend of fear and excitement bubbled in my belly.

Papa terrified me, but I wanted so badly to earn his approval.

"Shit," Mama whispered. "Go to your room. Don't come out until I tell you to."

"But I want a snack," I whined.

"Ogun! Go! This is not the time." Mama looked scared, and I hated it. It scared me when she was scared. That's why I went to my room. Not because I wanted to.

When I heard the door crash open, I scurried into my closet. In the darkness, I hid as Mama cried and Papa screamed.

"You leave me and you do it without my son, bitch!" Papa shouted. I didn't want to stay without my mama. I didn't understand why Papa would say that. There was more he said that I didn't hear.

Once the front door slammed and I heard Papa's bike start up, I crawled out of the closet and went to find Mama. She was curled up on the floor. Crying but quiet, she stared into space.

"Mama?" I whispered. Pushing her hair out of her face, I kneeled down to make her look at me.

"Ogun." She coughed, and blood came out. It ran onto her chin and the floor. "I told you not to come out."

"Mama, you're hurt." Fear swirled and churned inside me.

Except that time, it started to mix with something powerful. Something bigger than me and angry. So terribly angry.

The glass of water on the coffee table flew to the wall and shattered.

Startled, I jumped. Mama's eyes went wide, and she pushed herself up on her arms, then to sitting as she winced. Shaking hands grabbed my arms. "Ogun," she choked out.

That was the first time I knew my Papa might not be the man I thought he was. He'd been my hero until that day. Then again, what did a six-year-old know? That was also the first time I saw something that terrified me—and it wasn't my mother's battered face.

"Mama?" I questioned as my vision distorted. As if I was in a haze, I knew she held my hand and I knew she was calling my name, but I couldn't respond.

The room went dark around me, and only a small frame of light shone. It was like watching a movie. First, I saw my father drive a large knife into my mother's chest. Everything went black for a moment. Then, I saw my grandmother rushing me and my mother into a car. We ducked in the back seat, and I crouched on the floor while Mama lay across the seat, a large red mark on her white shirt.

We drove and drove until we met with men I didn't recognize. Everyone was talking, but I couldn't hear them. Then, everything got fuzzy.

Feeling disoriented, I blinked as a frown furrowed my forehead. My words sounded slurred even to my young ears. "Mama, Papa hurt you but Granmè is gonna take us away."

My mother's eyes went huge and she looked out the window. There was a man on a motorcycle with the same vest as my Papa. I'd seen him before, but I didn't know him. Mama made me stay in my room when Papa's friends came over.

"Get me my phone, Ogun," she whispered and pointed to her phone under the chair across the room. It took a few seconds for my arms and legs to work right but once they did, I scurried to bring it to her.

Whimpering, she scooted herself to lean against the couch. She put the phone to her ear, and I heard her say, "Ma, I need your help. It's Ogun. He saw something." Her eyes darted to me, then out the window.

The entire situation scared me, because I had no idea what was going on. Because I didn't know what else to do, I sat down next to my mother and curled into her side. Her arm wrapped around me, and we sat in silence.

A knock at the door sometime later brought my head up quickly. Glancing in fear toward the knock, I then looked to my Mama for guidance.

"Go see if it's Granmè," she said. Scrambling to my feet, I ran to the window and looked to the side to see the front porch. A wide grin took over my face as I squealed.

"Granmè!" With excited hands, I unlocked the handle and swung the door open. The woman who had helped raise me stepped into our home with a jovial wave to the man out front.

After she was inside and the door locked, she rushed to my mother. With worried eyes, I watched as she gently ran her hands over my mother. "Is Mama gonna be okay?" I asked, worry eating me alive.

"Yes, my sweet boy. Mama will be fine. Why don't you go have some of the cookies I baked you?" She motioned to the container she'd set on the table by the couch when she came in. Excited, I scooped it up and took it to the small table in the kitchen. If my grandmother said Mama would be okay, then it would be as she said.

Though I was busy stuffing my face, their words carried into where I sat.

"Ma, you need to get Ogun out of here." My ears perked up and my chewing slowed.

"I'm taking you both. I'll get your father and his boys to get you out of here. It's time, Julia. I've let this go on too long." My grandmother's harsh whisper carried further than she realized.

"Ma, Ogun is all that matters. He has the sight, I'm sure of it. But there's more. The glass…." She trailed off and I knew she was talking about the glass of water I knocked off the table. Though I didn't remember touching it.

A sharp intake of breath preceded my grandmother's muttering, and I wondered what she was saying as I slowly chewed the cookie.

"There is no time to waste. Are you able to pack a bag for yourself?" I heard my grandmother ask. Then I heard her say she would pack stuff for me.

My mother and my grandmother hid our bags after they were stuffed full. Then Mama and Granmè tucked me in. "You be a good boy, Ogun. There are powerful things coming in your future." Her soft hand feathered through my hair as she sat on the edge of my bed. Mama was sitting down by my feet with her hand resting on my ankle.

"Okay," I said, though I had no idea what she was talking about. They both kissed my head and closed my door on the way out.

I slept, but my dreams were plagued with dark images and a woman with long golden hair. I'd never seen her before, but she reached out to me, begging me to help her. No matter how hard I stretched my arm, I could never quite touch her fingertips.

When I woke up, Mama was cooking breakfast. She limped

a little and she had purple bruises on her face, arms, and around her neck. I didn't like it. I'd figured out that my father had done that to her.

"Mama, when I'm a papa, I won't hurt my ol' lady." I'd heard my father call her that, so I knew that's what she was to him.

She laughed her beautiful laugh and ruffled my hair. "You, young Ogun, won't have an ol' lady. You'll have a wife and a normal, loving family."

At the time, I hadn't understood what she was saying.

My father came home long enough to change his clothes. He paused outside my bedroom as I read a book. "Boy, what are you doing?"

"Reading, Papa! My teacher said I'm the best in our class!" My teacher's praise had made me very happy, but my papa didn't seem happy and my smile dimmed.

"Quit wasting your time on that shit. I'm not raising you to be a pussy. You hear me, boy?" His dark eyes narrowed as he stared down at me. It was hard to swallow, and I could only nod.

"Good. Come here." Nervous, I stood and walked toward him as he demanded.

He pulled a shiny gun from the back of his pants. He set it in my hand and I almost dropped the unexpected weight. His rough hand clutched the back of my neck and drove me down the hall to the kitchen where Mama was washing dishes.

At our footsteps, she turned toward us. When her eyes lit on what I was holding, I saw fear in her face.

"Giles, what are you doing?" she asked my father, but he ignored her and squeezed the back of my neck. I squeaked, and he shook me a bit.

"Shoot her," he said matter-of-factly. Confused, I blinked up at him.

"Papa?" I asked.

"You heard me, boy. Shoot. Her," he bit out in a quiet demand. My gaze flickered to my mother where she stood frozen with a dish towel in her hand.

"I don't want to do that," I said as my bottom lip quivered.

"Do it!" he screamed in my ear as I fought the tears that I instinctively knew he'd hate. My mother was shaking her head, and her mouth hung open but no words came out.

Pleading with my eyes, I looked at my father. Disbelief flooded me. I knew guns killed people because my dad let me watch movies with him where people would shoot other people. There would be lots of blood and then they died.

I didn't want my mama to die.

When I shook my head, he jerked the gun from me as he backhanded me, and I stumbled across the kitchen. Landing on my butt with a thud, I sniffled.

"Fucking pussy. See what you're raising?" He advanced on my Mama and held the gun to her head. My breath caught, and I froze.

"Giles, please," my mama begged.

Suddenly, he started laughing loud. He pulled the trigger, and it clicked but nothing happened. "Boom," he whispered, and a tear slipped from my eye.

"My boy is going to be a man, not a pussy like your *bastard* of a father," he said to her before he walked out the door and we heard his motorcycle start up and drive off.

Mama dropped to her knees and walked on them to me. She gathered me in her arms, and I cried like a baby.

"I'm so sorry, Mama. I'm so sorry," I said over and over.

"Shh, don't. It's okay, Ogun. It wasn't your fault. Go to your room. Okay?" She smoothed my hair and pressed a soft kiss to my forehead. I nodded and got up on shaky legs to do as she said. As I got to my door, she called down the hall, "I love you, Ogun."

"Love you too, Mama." I spent the rest of the day curled up on my bed with my ratty bear that I kept hidden between my bed and the wall. Papa said it was for babies, so I didn't let him see it. Mama had gotten it out of the trash the last time he threw it away and told me to keep him safe.

That next night, as my father was at his clubhouse doing God knew what, my grandfather who I'd seen very little of in my six years came to our home. He was a huge man, with a thick dark beard streaked with gray.

"Ogun, you're going to go far away with your mama. You'll be safe, but I need you to promise me you'll take good care of your mama, you hear?" he said as he crouched in front of me.

Nodding, I looked up at him through my long bangs. "Yes, sir," I said softly.

"Good boy." He stood and patted my head.

We got in the back seat of my grandmother's car. Mama lay on the seat, and I crouched on the floor.

"Mama? You're not bleeding," I said, confused. She sucked in a breath at the same time my grandmother did.

"Not everything you see will come to pass, sweet boy," my grandmother said, looking in the rearview mirror at me as I peeked over the seat. "Some things can be changed if you make the right choices. Never forget—Love always wins. Remember that, my boy. Over it all, love wins."

At the time, I had no idea what that meant.

It would be years before I understood.

ONE

Voodoo

"VOODOO"—GODSMACK

Approximately Twenty-Two Years Later...

"**I** know what you saw, boy. But you remember what I always told you." My grandmother's voice carried strong and powerfully over the phone line.

"Yes, I know, but I've seen it repeatedly, Granmè. I don't like it." My hand ran roughly through my hair.

"I'm being careful, and Jameson, that *beau diable*, has been checking on me. He even brought that pretty Sadie girl with him last time. I like her. She has a good soul, but she still carries a pain deep within her. They're good for each other. They will heal each other. You will have that one day," she said with certainty. I snorted in disbelief.

"Yeah, right." Zaka nudged his cold nose into my hand, and I glanced down at him. As I listen to my grandmother go on about her need for great-grandbabies, I stroked his thick, black fur. Another call chimed in, and I pulled the phone from my head to see who it was.

Seeing Raptor's name on my screen, I told her, "I have to go, Granmè."

It was her turn to snort. "You'll see, I'm right."

"Love you," I said, laughing. She replied in kind and we ended the call.

"Voodoo," I answered.

"Venom wants you at the clubhouse." His abrupt instruction caused me to roll my eyes.

"Would it kill you to say hello or acknowledge me before you bark out orders?" I grinned as I fucked with my VP.

He growled. "Get your ass over here. Church in thirty minutes."

Chuckling, I shoved my phone in my pocket. He'd hung up as soon as he'd finished talking. He wasn't an asshole; he just didn't have a lot to say over the phone. He hated them.

"Sorry, Zaka. I gotta go. You guard," I said as I ruffled his fur and grabbed the doorknob. He lay on the floor with his head on his paws, staring balefully at me. "You're pathetic," I mumbled with a hint of a smile to my lips.

Settling on my bike, I slid my shades on and scanned the neighborhood. It was a nice but unassuming neighborhood in Ankeny, Iowa—the heart of the country and home to the Royal Bastards MC in this neck of the woods.

Something deep in my soul missed the bayous of Louisiana, even though I'd only lived there for the first six years of my life. But this was home, and I truly wouldn't want to be anywhere else.

The ride to the clubhouse didn't take long, and I was thankful to see I wasn't the last one there. The last one into church had to clean the shitters. After the party we had the night before, I'd fucking pass.

"Voodoo, you freaky sonofabitch. How's it hanging?" Silver called out as I stepped into the dimly lit clubhouse.

Surprise hit me, because we hadn't been notified he was coming. He grabbed me in a tight embrace and patted my back as his giant of a prospect stood behind him silently watching everything. Prospects didn't join in church, so he'd be waiting outside the door when we went into the chapel.

Silver was the VP from our Detroit chapter. He called me freaky because of my beliefs, but rumor had it, he was certainly no angel.

"Hey, Silver. It's all good. What the hell are you doing down here?" I asked him as we stepped back and took seats at the large table. His smile dropped, and he looked over his shoulder at Venom.

"We're gonna discuss that in a minute, Voodoo. Where the fuck are Angel and Ghost?" Venom had barely gotten his question out when there was the sound of running feet. Angel and Ghost both slammed into the doorframe as they tried to burst through the door at the same time.

Ghost shoved at Angel and darted forward, tumbling into the nearest free seat. With a smug smile, he crossed his arms and gloated. "Angel's cleaning the shitters."

"Fuck you. You tripped me when I got off my bike, you asshole," Angel grumbled.

"No rules. So all's fair." Ghost gave him a smart-ass look. Angel glared at him as he tossed his phone in the basket outside the door with the rest of them. Ghost tossed his phone to Angel, who caught it midair. "Be a sweetie."

Angel flipped him off but tossed his phone in with the rest and closed the door.

"If you two don't knock your shit off and sit down, I'm gonna kick your goddamn asses." Venom growled. I tried not to smile as Ghost and Angel immediately calmed and sat quietly. No one wanted to push Venom too far and piss him off. It never ended well.

"Sorry, boss," Angel said as he pouted from his chair. Dark hair fell in his eyes, and he glowered.

"Now that you're all finally here, Silver has an offer for us. Listen up." Venom gave the floor to Silver, who'd been silently stroking his heavily graying beard.

"Thanks, brother," he said to Venom as he met each of our gazes one by one. "Due to the delicate nature of this request, it was unwise for us to relay it over open lines. We had a job request from Lorenzo De Luca. As I'm sure you know, he has retired to Texas, and his son Gabriel has taken the reins." We nodded, as this wasn't news. Lorenzo De Luca had been the head of the Sicilian mafia in Chicago until he'd retired. He'd been ruthless, but shrewd. His son Gabriel was no pushover, but from what we'd heard through the grapevine, he wasn't as brutal as his father had been.

Silver continued. "He told us he has a job that he wants us to handle. One that he knows Gabriel will never approve of. I don't know exactly what it is, but I can guess it has something to do with his youngest son being killed last month."

The death of De Luca's youngest son had made national news. There wasn't a soul in our world who didn't realize it was no accident.

"No disrespect, but what does that have to do with us down here?" Raptor questioned.

"The job involves a disposal and cleanup. Since that's your specialty and the job is in your backyard, that's why I'm here. He reached out to us specifically because of our history with them. We said we'd talk to you to see if you were interested, then let him contact you directly if that was the case. He said to tell you the compensation would be worth your while."

Raptor met Venom's gaze, and the silent communication that went on between them wasn't lost on us. None of us liked that Lorenzo De Luca had a job that was in our area, because the possible ramifications to that were endless.

Kicker raised a brow and stroked his red-and-gray beard. As our treasurer, he collected the money at our businesses and double-checked the books. Money was his language.

"We'll put it to the vote. I'll make a motion to talk to De Luca," Venom announced.

"I second that motion," replied Chains.

"All in favor of talking to Lorenzo De Luca?" It was a unanimous vote. Though I had a bad feeling about this whole thing, it didn't hurt to see what the guy wanted. Especially if the pay was as good as Silver was hinting at.

Raptor cleared his throat. "One other thing I need to mention is that the Bloody Scorpions have been nosing around in our area."

"What the fuck? They know they don't come up here." Venom's eyes flashed, and he growled in anger.

"Don't know. They don't seem to be doing anything, just riding through." Raptor leaned to the side in his chair, throwing an arm across the back.

"Everyone keep an eye out. You see them anywhere, you phone in immediately. We'll chase their asses all the way back to South Des Moines if we have to," Venom stated. Everyone agreed.

"You sticking around for the party tonight?" Venom asked Silver, who grinned and nodded.

"I wouldn't miss it for the world," he replied. "If you guys need any help with the Scorpions, you know we'd be here in a heartbeat."

"I sure appreciate that, Silver," Venom said. "Anyone got anything else? Or can we go get ready to party?"

Everyone around the table cheered for partying.

"Sure you're gonna be able to hang, old man?" Raptor teased. Silver was out of his seat in the blink of an eye, reaching across the table for Raptor's shirt. Venom's hand made a cracking noise as he slapped it around Silver's wrist to stop him. With his hands clenched, eyes narrowed, and nostrils flaring, Silver breathed heavily.

"Bro—it was a joke. Easy," Venom said quietly. He was a bit of an empath, to the point that he could calm someone by touching them. It was a little unnerving at times, but who was I to judge, considering my own abilities. He let go of Silver's wrist and sat in his seat.

"Seriously, I didn't mean anything by it," Raptor agreed, but I could tell he was ready to come unglued at a moment's notice. Those crazy amber eyes damn near glowed.

"My apologies," Silver said, but his jaw continued to tick. Slowly, he relaxed.

"We good, boys?" Venom asked. Though he appeared to be letting Raptor and Silver handle shit, I didn't miss the way he was ready to jump out of his chair again if need be.

"Yeah, it's all good," Silver grudgingly offered.

Venom gave Raptor an exasperated stare that clearly said he should've known better. Silver was a dude who would beat the fuck out of someone for calling him "old." Seriously, he was that sensitive about it, and we all knew it.

After Raptor shrugged in chagrin, Venom called an end to

church. He and a now calm Silver sat at the table, catching up. Things had been a little tense for a minute, and I'd worried that as my chapter's enforcer, I'd need to step in. It went against our code to lay hands on a brother without due cause, but we were all guilty of being a little edgy at times.

I pulled Shank, our SAA, to the side. "Hey bro, I need to take off for a bit, but I'll be back tonight. You need anything before I go? I don't want to interrupt while they're talking." I motioned to where Venom was laughing with Silver.

"Where you off to?" His dark eyes met mine as he pulled out his smokes and walked with me to the door. Once we were outside, he lit up and took a deep drag. The wrinkles on his face spoke of years in the sun.

"Got a vet appointment for Zaka. Shouldn't take long." I pulled my shades out of my inner pocket.

Shank nodded. "Hawk and your mama gonna come to the party tonight before they head down south?"

Shank was one of the older members and had been a prospect when Hawk, the man I called my dad, was a young member of the Ankeny chapter. Shank was a mean sonofabitch, but a loyal as hell brother.

"I doubt it. He and Mama were supposed to leave tonight for New Orleans; that's why he was excused from church. His truck was acting up. Now they're supposed to be leaving in the morning so they can check on Granmè and visit with the boys down there," I told him. He nodded to me as he blew out a cloud of smoke.

"Well, I'll sure as hell miss him, and I know everyone else will too," he said. My dad had been a member of the club since he was twenty-two and fresh out of the army. That was another reason I'd joined. It made it a bit of a family tradition. Hawk was

VP for several years, and only recently stepped down to "let the younger guys run shit," as he put it. The Royal Bastards were family, though and they'd probably always be that way for all of us.

By the time Mom and I got up to Iowa, Hawk was about twenty-five. It didn't take long for romance to blossom between the two of them, but he'd already stepped up and, along with the other members, was more of a father figure than my own had been for the first six years of my life.

"You have any idea what it is De Luca wants with us?" he asked me quietly as he took another drag on his smoke.

"None," I said with resignation.

"I guess we'll wait and see. You better get going. Catch you tonight," he said as he blew out the next cloud in a series of rings.

Giving him a chin lift, I walked to my bike, slid the shades on, and roared out of the lot with a wave to the brothers who were outside. The trip home took a bit longer than the way there because I got stuck behind a truck going slow as fuck.

Finally, I arrived at my house. Since I had to cage it to get Zaka to the vet, I pulled my bike into the garage. Zaka was raising hell when I shut the bike off. He recognized the sound of all of my vehicles and was always tripping out when I got home. If it was anyone else, he was quiet and stealthy until he knew if the person was friend or foe.

A giant, black, furry form barreled into me as soon as I stepped inside, head shoving into my stomach. "Sit," I said firmly, and he immediately dropped to his haunches.

Dark brown eyes stared excitedly up at me, and his entire body quivered with anticipation. The jet-black German shepherd waited anxiously for me to play. He was going to be pissed when he realized where we were going.

"Wanna go for a ride?" I asked him. His thick tail started wagging. I grabbed his leash and opened the door to the garage. "Load up!"

He bounded up into the Jeep and sat on the seat with his tongue lolling out of the side of his mouth. If I'd had the doors on, he would've been whining to get in. With a chuckle, I put his harness on him and latched it to the rigging I'd installed on the seat. If I was gonna have to cage it, I didn't want to feel enclosed, but I also didn't want to take the chance of my dog falling out.

As I backed out, I looked over my shoulder, and he did the same. When we started down the road, he seemed to smile as the wind blew his hair. I chuckled at his antics.

The minute he figured out where we were going, I knew. His mouth snapped shut, his ears lay back, his eyes narrowed, and he swung his head in my direction as if to glare.

"Oh, come on, buddy. It's not so bad. It's just a checkup." He blinked at me, and I swear he fumed. "You like the doc," I said with a grin. Hell, I liked the doc.

He stared me down the last few blocks until we parked and I shut off the Jeep. I unclipped the harness and jumped out of the driver seat.

"Let's go," I said as he continued to sit his big ass in the seat. I waited for him to get down. "Dammit, Zaka, come."

Still, he refused. "You are not winning this battle of wills, young man," I said as I rounded the hood. He sat there looking down his nose at me.

"Motherfucker," I muttered as I reached in and lifted his big ass out of the Jeep. He had to grunt and grumble as I did it, too. Because it was clinic policy, I clipped the leash to the harness.

When I started toward the door, he wouldn't budge.

"Oh, for crying out loud! It was a joke!" I said as I threw my arms out and leaned slightly toward him. He had the nerve to turn his head away.

Laughter sounded behind me, and I looked over my shoulder at the vet tech, Veronica, sticking her head out of the door. "Is he still mad from the last time, when you told him he was getting fixed?"

Palming my face, I nodded.

"Surely he didn't really understand that?"

I raised a brow in question. "You think not?"

"I know how to get him in." She gave me a teasing grin, chuckled, and slipped back inside.

"Now look what you're doing. You're making me look like a shitty owner. Like I can't control my own dog," I grumbled as I stood with my arms crossed. I gave the leash another tug and tried to coax him toward the door. He wouldn't budge.

"Zaka. Don't you want to come see me?" I didn't have to turn around. I knew exactly who had spoken, because my dick was hard.

My traitorous dog tipped his head to look around me. His big, fat tongue fell out of his mouth, and I rolled my eyes. "You're pathetic," I muttered, like I wasn't the one with a boner.

"Come, Zaka," she said, and he hopped his ass up and followed her in the clinic with me following along at the end of the leash like a putz.

This fucking dog.

She pointed to the scale, and he hopped right up and sat down. I wanted to choke him.

"Seventy pounds," she read off to the tech sitting at the front desk.

Then she stepped into an exam room, and Zaka followed her right on in. Once we were both in, she shut the door and held her hand out for him to sniff, even though it was apparent he knew exactly who she was.

"How's he been doing?" she asked me as she crouched next to him to love on my dog. I was more than a little jealous. Especially since I could see down the front of her red scrub top and her cleavage was screaming at me. When she looked up, her hazel gaze paused right at her eye level—my crotch. Then her cheeks flushed a little and she blinked up at me.

"Good. Unless he knows we're coming here." I smirked, and she grinned. She had no idea how bad I wanted to wrap her silky ponytail around my fist and pull her face into my cock. I shook off the visions that were beginning to form of her on her knees in front of me.

"I told you he was very intelligent," she said as she tried to pull in her smile.

"Well, I didn't expect him to understand what I was talking about," I said with exasperation. She chuckled and shook her head.

"I'm not so sure he knew exactly what you were saying, but he knew it wasn't something he'd like." I raised a brow at her, telling her what I thought of her deduction.

"Oh, really. Well, I think he did know exactly what I was saying."

Instead of replying to me, she returned her attention to my dog. "Don't worry, handsome. We won't touch the family jewels," she crooned to him, and I swear the fucker smiled at her and gloated toward me.

"So much for man's best friend," I mumbled. She tried not to laugh as she assessed him under the guise of scratching and petting him. She looked closely at his muzzle and his gums. Then she listened to him with her stethoscope and finished her exam. Once she was done, she stood up.

"Everything looks and sounds good. No signs of infection. Do you have any questions?" she asked as she wiped her stethoscope and hooked it over her neck.

"When are you going to go to dinner with me?" I asked with a half-smile.

Her eyes got big, and she quickly glanced back down to Zaka. "That wouldn't be appropriate, Mr. Dupré."

"Oh, come on, Doc. It's dinner. I'm not asking you to fuck me. Unless you're game, then it's not off the table." I gave her one of my best smiles, and Zaka actually helped a brother out and laid his head against her leg. His big brown eyes blinked innocently up at her, and I made a mental note to give him an extra biscuit when we got home.

"Jesus, Ogun," she mumbled in flustered shock, and I realized it was the first time she'd called me by first name.

"Is that a yes?"

TWO

Kira

"HOME SWEET HOME"—MOTLEY CRÜE

I never should have spoken his unusual name aloud. It was like summoning the dragon by speaking its name. He was dangerous—to my sanity and my well-being, and I was intelligent enough to realize that.

The problem was, he was also like the sun. Brilliant, bright, and intoxicating in his heat. So captivating that you wanted to stare at him and be close to him, even if you knew you'd get burned.

I cleared my throat. "Mr. Dupré," I began.

"I liked Ogun better. Unless you want to call me Voodoo," he interrupted. The sexy rumble of his voice was making it really hard to stay professional, but it was imperative that I did so. I wasn't an idiot. I'd seen him on his motorcycle wearing that leather vest. That was a life I didn't want any part of—no matter how tempting it might be.

"Mr. Dupré," I firmly reiterated. "You and your dog are my

clients. It would be highly inappropriate for me to have a relationship with you."

"I'm not asking for a relationship," he argued. "It's dinner. Di-nner. Food. With company at the same table. That's it."

I was a barely out of school vet. I'd gotten lucky when Dr. Moran hired me as the third vet. I'd done my internship in his clinic and he'd taken me under his wing. The last thing I wanted to do was screw shit up by dating a client. Well, technically, the client's owner.

Except I really wanted to. I'd been seeing Mr. Ogun Dupré come in with Zaka since he got the gorgeous German shepherd as a little puppy. The first time he showed up with the fluffy black bundle, I fought not to be a stuttering mess. Ogun was that good-looking.

Which was why I'd worked especially hard to stay professional. Not that it helped. Each time he came in, he asked me out, and each time it got harder to refuse him.

Ogun Dupré had been in for countless visits, because though Zaka was extremely intelligent, he was a naughty and inquisitive puppy. He'd severed a tendon squeezing through some construction materials, he'd gotten bit by another dog when he got loose, he'd gotten sick from eating the neighbors' plants, swallowed a sock, and that was only the major stuff.

This was a follow-up from his adventures with a porcupine. Poor thing had quills all through his muzzle, in his gums, and even one ear.

There was a knock on the door, then Veronica stuck her chestnut head in. "Hey, Doc, is it okay that I brought Sasha up to the front desk? She was raising holy h—um, a ruckus in the back." She gave a nervous grin to Ogun as she bit her lip, and of course he flashed her his beautiful smile.

"Hey, Veronica. How are things?" he asked her in that way-too-sexy voice of his. He came across as a broody grouch when I first met him, but he'd quickly warmed up to us in the office. New people, not so much.

I'd seen him in the grocery store and a few times around town. He always looked like he might set someone on fire with a look. I'd watched people take a wide berth around him in the store aisle and sit further away from him in restaurants. In a way, it made me feel bad for him, but he didn't seem bothered by it.

Before Veronica could answer him, I answered her.

"Sure, that's fine. Just be sure to hang on to her when we bring Zaka out," I instructed her. "Shut the door completely until we're done," I politely dismissed her. Not that I didn't like her; I simply didn't like to watch the flirting between her and Ogun.

When I turned back toward him, I jumped because he had silently moved to stand right in front of me. His one step forward sent me one step back until my back was against the door.

The teasing look had vanished, and in its place was that dark, heated gaze he so often had. The one that sent my heart rate into overdrive and shivers down my spine.

He slowly licked his bottom lip as his pale eyes stared into my soul. One hand reached up and grabbed the two ends of my stethoscope. Using it much like a lasso, he reeled me in. "What are you afraid of?"

"I—I, uh, it's not appropriate," I stuttered.

"Bullshit," he softly replied, causing his warm breath to feather across my cheek. "That's the only argument you ever have. I think you're afraid that dinner wouldn't be enough for *you*—that if I got a taste of those plush lips, I wouldn't stop. Then you'd go up in flames and there'd be no turning back."

It was unnerving that it seemed like he could read my mind. So of course, I denied it with a laughing scoff. "You're delusional!"

His lips curled again, but this wasn't his flirty smile. It was sinister, and oh so damn sultry it made a fine sheen of sweat break out over my upper lip. "If that's what helps you sleep at night."

My breath caught, and it took a moment to get myself together. With an overly bright smile, I took a deep breath and said, "Okay, well, Zaka looks great. I'll go and get his chart closed out."

With a mirthless chuckle, he shook his head. "You know I'm not giving up."

"You should," I said on a heavy sigh.

"But I won't," he smugly replied before stepping back far enough to let me open the door. The scent of his cologne followed me as I left the room, and I gave a silent sigh.

I was passing on the information regarding Zaka to the receptionist to enter in the computer when Sasha jumped up and rushed past me. I tried to grab her collar, but she was fast.

"Sasha!" I called but she was already focused on her target. Shit balls.

It all happened so quickly, I barely had time to move.

Ogun was coming out of the exam room with Zaka by his side, and Sasha was barreling down on him. My heart constricted when Zaka's ears folded and his body tensed.

To my extreme horror, Sasha grabbed onto Zaka's ear and bit it right as I grabbed for her. Blood started going everywhere. Everyone was all hands on deck, worried there would be a dog fight.

"Whoa! Hold up there, little fella," Ogun said as he grabbed her collar. There was no way he could put enough distance between the two dogs if needed.

I grabbed her collar, and my hand brushed his as I pulled her away. "Sasha! Release!"

Lo and behold, she listened.

"Bad girl!" I scolded her after she sat. "I called your name, young lady. Mr. Dupré, I'm so sorry! If you'll take him back in the exam room, I'll check his ear."

Sasha jumped up and was twisting in my hand, trying to get free to get back toward what she saw as her new friend. "Veronica!" I called. She'd promised to hold on to her if she was at the desk with her.

I heard running coming from the back, and Veronica arrived, breathless. "Oh my gosh, I'm so sorry! I had to run Mrs. Turnbow's chihuahua to the back because she got out of the kennel somehow. I thought I'd be back before he came out."

"Take Sasha for me." Though she was fighting to get loose, she was wagging her tail and whining to get back to Zaka.

Ogun had returned to the room with his dog, and the rest of us tried to clean up the mess before another customer came in and it looked like we'd slaughtered an animal in the small lobby.

"You go take care of Zaka, I'll get this," Veronica offered. Thankful for her return from putting my now howling dog in her crate, I pushed the loose tendrils of hair out of my face.

Ugh, I must look a mess.

Hurrying into the room, I closed the door firmly. "Mr. Dupré, I'm really very sorry."

"Did you get hurt?" he asked as he stared at me. Looking down, I realized I'd gotten blood all over my arm.

"Oh! No, that was from Zaka. Let me wash up, and I'll take a look at him." Mortification swallowed me alive as I scrubbed my hands and arm.

"I think it was just a lucky bite. Is she yours?" he asked as he held a paper towel to Zaka's ear. Zaka was being remarkably good through all this.

Then it hit me. He could sue me over this. *Shit.*

"She is," I reluctantly agreed as I checked his dog's ear. The bleeding had stopped, but there was a small puncture wound. "I think it will heal closed, but I can suture it if you want."

He laughed, and I looked at him in surprise. "It will be fine. I'm sure it will grow shut, and it will match his porcupine piercings." It was the opposite ear of the porcupine quill holes. They had grown shut nicely, but a few spots left some tiny scars.

"Sasha is up to date on all of her shots," I assured him. "I can get you a copy of her shot records."

"No need. How old is she?" he asked as he crouched down next to me and scratched his dog's neck.

"She's six months old," I replied as I finished cleaning the small wound. His proximity was doing really crazy things to me. I desperately wanted to ask him to back up, but then I'd be giving away that he affected me.

"She's beautiful. I didn't know you had a German shepherd. Did you get her because of Zaka?" That disarming grin came out to play again, and I had to look away.

"Of course not," I said a little emphatically. I'd wanted one my whole life, but my father hated dogs. However, Ogun's dog had been my driving force to finally get one.

"Mmm-hmm. Whatever you say." His tone was teasing, and he'd seemed unconcerned about the incident, but I needed to know.

"Are you going to sue me?" My teeth tugged on my lower lip, and I pushed my hair that had escaped my ponytail behind my ears.

"What? Don't be ridiculous. It was a simple accident. I don't think she's mean, nor did she intend to hurt him." At his words, I relaxed.

My relaxation was short-lived.

"But you could ensure there are no hard feelings by going out with me tonight," he said with a smug smile. My mouth fell open at his audacity.

"Are you blackmailing me?" My eyes were big with disbelief.

The laughter that escaped him was rich and rare. I'd heard him chuckle, but the boisterous laugh curled my toes and was infectious enough, I had to fight giving him a sappy smile of my own.

"Let's call it friendly persuasion," he finally replied. I shot him a look that said I wasn't amused. Looking him in the eye was a mistake with the minimal space between us, because I was mesmerized by his pale blue eyes. The strong lines of his jaw, the bold slash of his brows. Everything about him called to me.

Blinking rapidly, I broke the spell and cleared my throat. Then I stood to put some distance between us.

"I'll pick you up at six," he said, and I gasped.

"But I didn't say yes!" I exclaimed.

He gave me that sultry smile again and headed to the door. Pausing with his hand on the knob, he turned to me. "You didn't have to. You have my number in my file. Text me your address."

The room was vacated by the frustrating man and his beautiful beast as I sat reeling. Hiding out in the exam room until I knew they were gone, I pretended to be cleaning.

"That's my job," Veronica said from the doorway. I glanced her way to see her cheerful grin.

"I know. But I don't have another client, and it's almost closing time." We closed early on Saturday.

The bell on the door chimed, and Dr. Moran came in. He'd

been on a farm call this morning for an unexpected and difficult equine delivery. He was the only large animal vet in this practice.

"Kira," he boomed in his deep voice. "Thank you so much for holding down the fort for me today."

"It was nothing, considering how light the load was today." We discussed the various animals that had come in, including Zaka. Mrs. Turnbow came in for her dog, and he briefly chatted with her. Once she'd left, I finished filling him in on the day's few patients. The whole time, I nervously debated asking him about my situation.

"Is everything okay?" he asked, able to read me well. After ensuring Veronica and the receptionist were out of earshot, I fidgeted and then looked him in the eye.

"Um, what is the policy here for personal interactions with our customers?" It was suddenly difficult to swallow, and I desperately wanted a drink. My gaze dropped to my shoes.

His knowing chuckle had my head whipping up to look at him. Kindly, he asked, "Let me guess, Voodoo Dupré?"

Shock had me blinking owlishly. "How could you possibly know that?"

"Well, for one, I just finished talking to him in the parking lot. But other than that, I've seen the way he looks at you when he's in with that big beast of his." He gave me a soft smile, and I cleared my throat nervously.

"There is no policy. We're a small family-owned clinic. However," he suddenly got serious, "it can make for a sticky situation later if things don't work out. And Voodoo is… well, I've known him since he moved here as a little boy. He's a force, to be sure, but he's always seemed a little broken. I don't want you getting hurt."

Dr. Moran had been a great mentor, and I valued his

opinion. As well as his concern. The last thing I wanted was for him to worry about me though. What he didn't know was that I was a lot tougher than he was aware.

"It's only dinner." I shrugged like it was no big deal.

"Hmm," he hummed knowingly before he cupped my shoulder with a callused and wrinkled hand. His wizened eyes searched deep in my own. "Just don't expect too much from him."

With that, he left the room to go back to his office where Mrs. Moran waited for him so we could close up and everyone could go home.

As I grabbed my tote and my naughty puppy, I looked at the sticky note I'd jotted his number on. It was only dinner, I repeated to myself for the millionth time.

Except the truth was, I had a sense that he was right.

This had the potential to combust. I could feel it in my bones.

I only hoped I'd survive the blaze.

THREE

Voodoo

"BLACK NO. 1 (LITTLE MISS SCARE-ALL)"—TYPE O NEGATIVE

Snuffing the candles, I rose from my small altar and set the small silver blade on the worn wood. The scent of the herbs that had been burning clung to my clothes. For the first time in a long time, my inner demons were quiet and peace enfolded me in a heavy cloak. It was unusual, and I had to wonder what was behind it.

Though I knew. Deep inside, I knew.

It was her.

Dr. Kira Baranov always stilled the beasts that lurked in the darkest corners of my soul. Simply being in her presence was like breathing clean air after a fire. It was part of the reason I'd relentlessly pursued her each time I'd taken Zaka to see her.

I doubted it would last; it rarely did. My whole life, I'd turned to various vices to quiet the ugliness inside me. They all worked temporarily to distract and calm the churning anger I kept tightly leashed.

Noting the time, I left the basement, quickly showered, dressed, grabbed my keys, wallet, pistol, and finally shrugged on my cut. I'd been proud to earn the right to wear the skull with the crooked crown, and not a day went by that I wasn't. Of course, that was much to my mother's disappointment.

Truthfully, she didn't have a lot of room to bitch. She'd ended up falling for one of the members who'd been tasked with getting us away from New Orleans and to a new life. It may not have been the life she wanted for me, but it was in my blood.

My sperm donor may have been a piece of shit, but my grandfather had been a Royal Bastard and so had the man I considered my father. The one who taught me how to be a man.

"Guard," I told Zaka as I went to the door of the garage. After nine months, he was finally trustworthy enough to leave loose in the house. At least there weren't any porcupines in there for him to try to play with. I'd made sure the doggie door was secured after he'd gone out to do his business, to be safe.

He pouted with his head on his paws.

"I have a date with Doc," I said. His ears perked up, and he lifted his head and tilted it to the side as if he understood. His thick tail began to thump. I chuckled and went out, closing the door behind me.

Before I started my bike, I shot her a text.

Me: Make sure you're wearing jeans and boots. We're taking my bike.

Doc: uh ok. Do u have a helmet for me? I don't have one.
Me: I got you
Doc: Why do I feel like I'm gonna regret this?
I laughed out loud.
Me: You won't
Doc: You're pretty sure of that

Me: See you soon

Tucking my phone into an inside pocket of my cut, I strapped my helmet to the sissy rest I'd latched on as soon as I'd gotten home with Zaka—I'd been that confident she'd text.

The bike roared to life, and I wracked the pipes as I rolled out of the garage. After hitting the remote to close the door, I took off toward the address she'd texted me earlier.

She lived in a nice area with newer, but modest homes.

I backed up to the curb in front of her house. I'd barely swung my leg over the seat when she rushed out of the house. Giving her a suspicious look, I wondered why she seemed in such a hurry. Especially considering how reluctant she'd been to go out with me.

I took a second to appreciate the tight jeans that hugged her every curve and the tall back boots that encased her calves like gloves. Stifling a groan at the way the long-sleeved T-shirt she wore stretched over her perfect tits, I fought the need to adjust my junk.

"Where's the helmet?" she asked as she held out her hand.

Crossing my arms, I narrowed my eyes and asked her, "What's the rush?"

Wide hazel eyes darted to the house, then back to me. That had me raising a brow.

The door flew open, and a woman with brunette hair stuck her head out the door. "I see you trying to sneak out, Kira!"

Raising both brows, I looked to her for an explanation. Her shoulders sagged.

"Come on, I'll never hear the end of it if I don't introduce you two." She trudged back to the house.

The brunette had a smug grin and her arms crossed as she waited on us. We stepped onto the porch, and she reached a hand out.

"Hello. I'm Geneva, Kira's roommate. And you are?" She had a remarkably firm handshake for a woman.

"Voodoo," I replied.

"Voodoo? Jesus, did your mom not like you?" She had spunk, and I appreciated that, but I wasn't giving her my given name, because as far as I was concerned, she didn't need it.

"My momma liked me just fine." Daring her to pursue what was none of her business, I left it at that.

"So you're one of those bikers I see riding around town, huh?"

"Oh my God, Geneva. Enough," Kira said in exasperation. It caused me to chuckle.

"What?" she asked Kira. "I just wanted to know if they were like that TV show!"

My eyes rolled, because I couldn't help it. While there might be some shit from that show that was uncannily accurate, most was highly fictionalized.

"Not quite, Geneva," I replied.

"Well, take my girl here for a real good ride. She needs it." I couldn't help it, I laughed at her innuendo.

"Okay, time to go!" Kira cut in. She grabbed my arm and tugged. There was no way she could've moved me on her own, but I was anxious to get going, so I let her.

"Nice to meet you, Geneva," I said over my shoulder as we moved toward my bike.

"Okay, can we go now?" Kira had exasperation written all over her face.

"Sure," I said as I grabbed the helmet and unhooked the bungee from it. Pleased that she'd braided her hair so it didn't tangle, I placed the helmet on her head.

"I can do that," she fussed.

"I've got it," I insisted, because it gave me a reason to touch her. Her skin that my fingers brushed was silky soft, and I longed to explore every inch of it.

Once it was strapped on as tight as it would go, I got on and motioned for her to climb on behind me. She looked uncertain, so I told her how to get on. She was surprisingly adept.

"Have you ridden?" I asked as I looked over my shoulder.

"Yeah."

"The way you acted, I thought you'd never been on a bike."

"It wasn't that" was her evasive response.

"Hmm." Letting it drop, because I didn't like to think of her on a bike with someone else, I started the engine, and we pulled away from her house. Once we got on the main road, I hooked her thigh with my hand and tugged on her to scoot forward.

The heat from between her legs hit me like a ton of bricks, and my goddamn cock jumped again. It was a bit of torture for me, but worth every second.

We hopped on highway 69 and got off on First. I pulled in to Cazador and parked. Once I'd shut off the bike, I helped her off.

"You good with Mexican?" I asked as she was removing the helmet. It hadn't occurred to me to ask in advance, because I wasn't really a dating kind of guy. The mechanics of a date were a little foreign to me.

"Yeah," she said, and she bit her lip. I took the helmet and hung it on the handlebar. She looked from the helmet to me.

"Won't someone steal it?"

Huffing out an amused snort, I shook my head. "Not if they know what's good for them. Trust me, no one will mess with anything on this bike."

She obviously didn't understand the 1% sticker and the SYLRB decal.

Looking dubious, she walked with me when I placed a hand on her lower back and guided her to the doors. For a moment, I paused and glanced around. She gave me a questioning look. The feeling of being watched diminished, and I continued into the restaurant.

Once we were seated and looking over the menu, she seemed to fidget nervously.

"Everything okay?" I asked.

The waitress came and got our drink order. Surprisingly, she ordered a margarita and a glass of water. "Water for me," I told the waitress, who assured us she'd be back for our order.

"Well?" I prodded. She sighed.

"Look, Voodoo, Ogun, whatever you want me to call you, I don't know what I'm doing going out with you. You're everything I don't need to be mixed up in—everything I've tried to get away from." She hesitated.

"What are you trying to get away from? Are you in trouble?" Never in a million years would I have thought she'd have skeletons in her closet.

"No, nothing like that." She fidgeted nervously. "I'm worried that if this goes badly, it will affect our professional relationship at the clinic. Dr. Moran said there was no policy against us going out but to be cautious."

Stiffening slightly, I took exception to him warning her away from me.

"Don't get me wrong," she said. "He didn't tell me not to go out to dinner with you, but he said he hoped it wouldn't cause tension in the clinic if it didn't work out."

Relaxing, I nodded. "I get it. But don't worry. I'm mature enough not to be an ass." Maybe a bit of a lie, because I could be a real dick when I wanted to be. In fact, most people found me pretty intimidating, but she made me feel lighter. A little more human.

The waitress dropped off our drinks, took our order, and left again.

She appeared to ponder on the situation. "Okay. But you need to know that I'm not looking for a relationship. My life is pretty busy right now."

"That's perfectly fine with me. I'm not much of a relationship kind of guy either. But I like you, and I'd like to get to know you more. Hang out. Whatever."

She stiffened slightly when I said I wanted to get to know her. Most people might not have noticed it, but I was extremely adept at reading people.

"Mmm," she said before she took a sip of her margarita.

"How do you feel about stopping by the clubhouse after this?" I asked her, gauging her reaction.

"Umm, like your motorcycle club hang out?" Nervous energy poured from her. "Who all will be there?" she asked as she trailed a finger through the condensation on her glass.

Not sure who she was worried about being there, I opted for the truth. "The club members, maybe an ol' lady or two, likely several, uh, club girls."

She raised a dark blonde brow. "Club girls?"

Pushing on my bottom lip with my tongue, I debated how to describe them. Any other time, I wouldn't have hesitated, but she was different. "It's probably exactly what you're thinking."

"So chicks that sleep with all the guys?" she bluntly questioned. Her finger tapped the side of the glass as she stared in my eyes.

"You could say that," I replied with a shrug. Leaning back in the booth, I took in every minute thing about her, trying to see how bold she would be.

"Chicks that you sleep with?"

"I have."

"Oh," she murmured as she took a sip of her drink again. "So if, um, we…." She stuttered and trailed off without finishing her thought.

Deciding I wasn't going to beat around the bush because it wasn't in my nature, I sat up and tapped her hand that rested on the table. "Hey. I'm a little new to this dating shit. Though we said we weren't going to pursue a relationship, per se, if we did take this further, I wouldn't be fucking anyone as long as we were fucking." And I was honest enough with myself to admit that I'd wanted to fuck her from the first time I laid eyes on her.

"Holy shit," she huffed.

"Too blunt?" I raised a brow as the corner of my mouth lifted.

"No." She cleared her throat and wiggled in her seat. My head cocked as I studied her. Though she may have been trying to hide it, I could literally smell her arousal. The pheromones she exuded were off the charts, and my dick jumped against the zipper of my jeans. If I thought for one second she'd be up for it, I'd say fuck the food and take her back to my place.

"Good."

The food came, and we ate with small talk interspersed between bites.

"So I find it interesting that you have a female German shepherd."

"Why?" she asked after washing her food down with more of her margarita.

"It's just interesting. You have a female, I have a male. Do you intend to fix her?"

"I'd not planned on it. She has champion bloodlines."

"So does Zaka," I added.

"I'm aware."

"Really?"

She cleared her throat. "Okay. Honesty?"

"Always."

"It has always been a dream of mine to have a GSD, but my father would never allow me to have a dog. However, I'd be lying if I said I didn't consider breeding Sasha to Zaka." Her cheeks flushed a soft pink.

"So it's okay for our dogs to fuck, but not us?" I teased. She gasped and quickly looked around to see if anyone had heard me. Her hand shot out and squeezed mine.

"Shh!" she whispered in dismay, but I barely heard her.

As I sat there in a bustling Mexican restaurant, I had a vision that would change the course of everything.

FOUR

Kira

"DAYLIGHT"—MAROON 5

When I grabbed Ogun's hand, he froze and his eyes went slightly unfocused. It only lasted for a few seconds, but it left me feeling shaken and wondering if he'd had a minor seizure.

"Are you okay?" I asked when he paled and fell back against the back of the booth. He blinked rapidly and shook his head.

"Jesus," he whispered before taking my margarita and swallowing the last of it.

"Ogun?" I questioned. He didn't look good.

"I'm… uh, I'm good." He didn't look it, but his color was returning as his gaze locked on mine. It was impossible to stop staring into his crystalline eyes.

We both jumped a little when the waitress came up to the table. She made to leave the bill, but Ogun pulled cash out of his wallet, handed it to her, and said, "Keep the change."

"You didn't even look at the bill," I said in exasperation. He shrugged and stood up.

"It was enough," he said. I rolled my eyes.

"I wasn't implying you shorted her. You likely gave her a tip as big as our bill."

Again, he shrugged. When he held out a hand, I reached up and allowed him to help me out of the booth. As I stood, he pulled me so close to him, his heat washed over me in waves.

"Ogun?" I breathlessly questioned. He was acting strange, but it was affecting me in the oddest way.

"You never answered me. You up for stopping by the clubhouse?" he gruffly asked.

"If we're not dating, wouldn't that send the wrong message?"

"How?"

"Um, you taking me into the sanctity of your clubhouse to meet your gang?"

That drew a dark chuckle from his gorgeous lips. "It's a club, not a gang. And I can bring anyone I damn well please to a party."

"Okay," I murmured.

Suddenly feeling like things were quickly escalating into something neither of us was truly prepared for, I took a shuddering breath. My eyes searched his, looking for answers to the uncertainty that plagued me.

More gently than I would've ever thought him capable, he cupped my cheek, and my breath hitched. It was like a jolt of something unnatural, but not the least frightening, shot through me. Those pale blue eyes were captivatingly hypnotic.

Without another word, he dropped his hand, grabbed mine, and led me back out to his bike.

Still silent, he handed me the helmet. I put it on with shaking fingers, and before I knew it, we were headed down the road.

My mind was in such a jumble, I didn't pay attention to where we were going. The feel of his firm muscles under my hands was driving me to distraction, along with the intoxicating scent of his cologne mixed with the leather of his vest. Any hope I had of keeping my wits about me blew away with the passing breeze.

"We're here," he said as he tapped my thigh. Blinking, I realized we'd not only arrived, but he'd parked the bike at the end of a row of others.

With trembling limbs, I climbed off and tried to ignore the large group of people staring at us. The looks on their faces ranged from shock, to smugness, to straight-up anger. The last was on a woman with bright red hair and more skin than clothing showing.

Unbraiding my surely messy hair, I finger combed it, hoping it looked somewhat presentable.

The heat of his hand on my lower back was another jolt, and I moved forward. He left it resting there as we approached the group.

"You want something to drink?" he asked as he motioned toward several metal water troughs full of ice.

"Is there a bottle of water?" I asked through incredibly parched lips. Licking them in an attempt to moisten them, I caught his gaze. His pupils were dilated, and lust was blatant in them.

Swallowing with increasingly difficult effort, I saw his lips tilt in a semblance of a smile. He plunged his hand into the ice, fished around a bit, and came out with three longnecks grasped in his fingers.

"Beer, beer, or beer?" He held them up.

"Um, beer?" I said with a laughing shake of my head as I grabbed an import.

"Good choice," he chuckled. He dropped one back into the

ice, then used one of the chunky rings on his fingers to pop off both lids.

"Thanks," I said with an eye roll and a smile.

"I want to introduce you." He grabbed my hand and pulled me back toward the crowd. My heart hammered as I took in all the rough-looking bikers. Except, I'd be lying if I said they weren't attractive. Well, most of them.

We stopped in front of a burly guy with a lush salt-and-pepper beard. His vest said "Venom" and "President." The two guys next to him both had tabs that said "Vice President," and I was confused. Then I saw that they had different places on another tab. The guy with a thick silver beard and slicked-back hair to match was obviously from Detroit—and coincidently, his name was "Silver," according to his name tab.

"Pres, I'd like you to meet Kira." Venom's gray-blue eyes seemed to go green, and I was mystified at how they'd seemed to change colors before my eyes.

He took the hand I offered and raised it to his lips with the snake bite piercings, but he left me feeling much more relaxed after shaking his hand. The way he held me and kissed my hand wasn't inappropriate, but Ogun's hand that rested on my lower back clenched my side, and I jumped a little.

"It's a pleasure, Miss Kira," Venom, the man Ogun called "Pres," said with a humorous glance at Ogun.

"And this is my VP, Raptor, and our Detroit chapter VP, Silver," Ogun went on with the introductions. If looks could strip you naked, the man he called Silver was a pro at it. He gave me such a heated stare as he trailed his blue eyes from my head to my toes that I shivered. He gave me a knowing smile, and Ogun gripped me again.

"Nice to meet you both," I said as I shook first Silver's, then

Raptor's hand. Neither did anything inappropriate, but Raptor did give Ogun a strange look before his oddly light brown eyes returned to me.

His brown hair was closely cropped with a messy upsweep of the front. He was ruggedly attractive, as were the others. His eyes narrowed on me, leaving me feeling almost naked. Exposed.

"Do I know you from somewhere?" he asked me. When I realized Ogun was squeezing me again, I also realized I was still holding Raptor's hand.

"Oh!" I said as I released his hand, and he gave a soft chuckle. "I'm a vet where Og—uh, Voodoo brings his dog, Zaka."

"Hmm, maybe I need to get a dog," he said with a flirty grin.

That time, I was pretty sure I heard Ogun growl. The three men broke out in laughter, and I glanced from face to face in confusion. While I didn't know the inside joke, I got the feeling they were messing with Ogun somehow.

"We'll see you guys in a bit," he grumbled as he led me over to another small group of guys sitting under the trees in lawn chairs.

"Hey, Voodoo! Who's this beauty, and where have you been hiding her?" a very blond man asked with a big grin.

"Jesus fucking Christ," he muttered next to me. "Kira, this asshole is Ghost, that dickwad is Angel, Croc's the fuckstick, then that asswipe is Chains, and next to him is Phoenix, the fucktard."

They all laughed except the one they called Chains. He silently drank his beer as he watched me and Ogun.

"Uh, hi," I stuttered. "I'm feeling the love."

That caused them to laugh even more, and Ogun actually chuckled softly next to me. Even Chains had a half smile.

"It's all good. If we weren't fucking with each other, we might wonder if there was any love at all," the one he called Angel said.

Ogun brought me around and introduced me to several other guys. I knew I'd never remember their names, because my brain was already on overload. All in all, there were about fifteen or more guys there, plus the scantily clad women.

There was an older guy who had his arm around the shoulders of a woman with a bandana on her blonde hair. Her name was Helen, and she seemed really sweet. They referred to her as the man's ol' lady, which I assumed was something special. They were with several of the older guys.

Unlike Geneva, I'd never watched any of the motorcycle shows. I'd never had time. Vet school was demanding as hell. Now at twenty-seven years old, I was finally feeling like I could have a life. Yet, I had no life.

"So what do you think?" he asked, pulling me out of my thoughts.

"Well, it's different?" I didn't mean it to come out as a question.

"Different good, or different bad?" he asked as he lifted the bottle to his lips to hide the slight lift of his sexy lips. He was sinfully gorgeous, and I was beginning to have thoughts about him that I knew were a bad idea.

Being far from drunk, I couldn't blame it on the alcohol, but something crazy hit me, and I bit my lip. Then I insanely said, "Maybe a little of both."

My eyes trailed from his beautiful eyes to the broad shoulders, and down the abs his tight T-shirt hinted at beneath the leather vest. Blatantly obvious, I paused on his zipper before finishing the beer in my hand.

I couldn't be sure, but I thought Ogun swore under his breath.

The sky was darkening, and the party seemed to be picking

up steam. It had gone from people standing around in groups, casually drinking, to someone cranking the music up and some risqué behavior.

Behavior that was oddly turning me on.

I hadn't realized how engrossed I was in watching one of the women on her knees in front of the guys in the lawn chairs until a hot breath blew across my ear. "You like watching?"

It dawned on me that my eyes had been locked on Chains as the woman gave him head. My face burned with both mortification at being caught staring and with how hot it made me.

"Do you have a bathroom I can use?" I asked suddenly. My voice was breathless, and I tried to ignore the husky chuckle that he released across my neck.

"Sure. This way," he said as he led me into what looked like a large metal building. I'd expected it to be a shop, since the place was out on the edge of a farm. Inside, it couldn't have been further from a shop. There was a large open space with couches scattered around, an oval bar in the center, and tables that surrounded it.

The high ceiling spanned the entire building, but it appeared to be well-insulated and ended at one end where a wall had been constructed. A set of stairs went up in the center. We headed in that direction.

When I tried to go into one of the two doors next to the stairs that said *restroom*, he tugged my hand. "Trust me. You don't wanna use either of those."

Confused, I looked over my shoulder as he guided me down a hall under the stairs that I hadn't noticed at first. There were a couple of closed doors, but we passed them. The short hall came to a T, and we took a right.

It was almost like walking down a hotel hall with doors on

either side. At the third door on the left, he stopped and pulled out his keys. After unlocking the door, he swung it open, flipped on the light, and motioned for me to go in.

It was like a dorm room. A bed with a dark comforter, a single nightstand, a dresser with a huge mirror, flat-screen TV mounted to the wall, and a scarred-up desk with a basic office chair.

"Is this where you live?" I asked him as I checked out the sparse furnishings.

"When I need to stay here," he said from where he leaned on the doorframe. His heated gaze followed my every movement. "Bathroom is through that door."

"Oh. Thanks," I said before rushing in and closing the door. Leaning on the back of it for a moment, I tried to calm my racing heart.

Jesus. What have I gotten myself into? Not that I hadn't seen worse growing up, but it hadn't affected me like it had outside. Then, I'd been able to ignore it. Now, I'd found myself unable to look away and I'd been incredibly turned on.

After several large breaths, I finished my business and washed my hands in the pedestal sink. Taking a second to check out the small space, I realized it was utilitarian, but efficient. Shower, no tub, small cabinet between the toilet and small sink, mirror over the sink. No decorations or personal touches.

Taking a peek in the cabinet, I saw a stack of neatly folded towels and washcloths. A razor, toothbrush, toothpaste, and travel size of cologne were all that spoke of someone actually staying in there.

Through the frosted shower door, I could see what was likely a bottle of shampoo and another bottle. That was it. No personalization in the small room, either.

Figuring I'd been in there long enough, I opened the door.

Ogun sat in the office chair doing something on his phone but looked up as soon as the door swung open. Without a word, he slipped it inside his vest. My eyes darted to the closed door and back to the intense man who was standing.

"It's not locked. If you want to go, feel free," he said in a tone that dared me to stay.

This ridiculously out of character part of me wanted things I shouldn't. It wanted him to unleash the beast I could see simmering in his eyes. It was a wild and fleeting thought that I assumed was mine alone.

Or I did until his hand shot out, spanning the front of my throat. His grip was firm, but not painful. Panic slithered through me for a second before his gaze dropped to my mouth, which had parted on a gasp.

He pulled me toward him, and our lips met in a demanding kiss. It was one I was fully and brazenly participating in.

And it was so incredibly good. Mind-blowing.

When he broke free and dropped his head to rest his forehead on mine, I reached up to grasp the arm that still held me.

"What are you doing?" I whispered and swallowed, knowing he could feel my throat move.

"Kira." He said my name like it was a prayer. "I've never been one to beat around the bush before. You wanna fuck? Or you wanna go back out there and drink?"

Slightly stunned, I stared at him slack-jawed. "Are you serious?"

What I intended to come out as indignant, came out with a crack to my voice and tremulous.

"Baby, I'm serious as a heart attack." His eyes were so dilated, they appeared dark. It was the first thing that gave away the level of his desire. The other was the way he seemed to be losing his control.

Wavering between what I was certain was the right choice and the one I *wanted* to make, I searched his eyes. Finally, I let my better judgement go by the wayside and pushed forward against the palm of his hand until my lips crashed to his again.

That time, it was a fierce clash of wills as we both jockeyed for the lead in what was a frighteningly passionate race. Our tongues twirled, stroked, and twisted against each other's as his taste left me spellbound. The hand around my neck squeezed minutely, causing my head to swim a bit.

With a growl, he released my neck, crouched slightly, lifted me, and caused my legs to instinctively wrap around his hips. The thick rod between his legs was by no means subtle as he ground it to that sensitive spot between mine.

"Oh!" I gasped as I shamelessly found myself on the verge of an orgasm.

My head fell back a bit with each step he took. He took advantage of that moment to trail bites and kisses along the column of my throat.

A needy moan escaped me. Too late, the voice of reason tried to rear its ridiculous head, so I shoved it back down. There would be time enough for it later. Better to suffer regret than to regret not doing it when I had the chance. Even if this was all we ever had, I'd always have the memories.

And something told me, with this man, those memories were going to be life-altering.

FIVE

Voodoo

"THE LIGHT"—DISTURBED

Normally, I was efficient when it came to sex. No unnecessary foreplay. No kissing. No emotions.

With Kira, that all went out the window, and I wasn't sure how to process that.

I'd reached the edge of the bed and reluctantly broke free from the spell of her kiss. Setting her on her feet, I framed her face in my hands. "I want you naked in that bed in ten seconds or I'm ripping those clothes off you."

The glazed look left her eyes. She blinked and paused. Half expecting her to back out, I was shocked when she actually whipped her clothes off in record time and tossed them in the chair.

She jerked the top linens back but paused. "Are these clean?" she hesitantly asked as she looked over her shoulder at me.

I couldn't help the laughter that escaped as I studied the prefect curve of her ass. "Yeah. They're clean. I haven't stayed here in several days, and I changed them before I left last time. I don't stay here often because of Zaka."

She frowned, and I knew she was wondering if I'd been in the bed with someone else. Not wanting her to change her mind, I grabbed the back of her neck, spun her around, and kissed her again.

Anything that had happened before her didn't matter, but I knew she wouldn't see it that way.

"Get that gorgeous ass in the bed," I growled against her lips as I broke free.

Once I knew she was doing as I said, I started to undress. My cut, I hung on the back of the chair; the rest went to the floor.

Unashamed of my nakedness, I walked to the edge of the bed. Her caramel-apple gaze was staring at my full-mast cock with a perfect blend of trepidation and hunger. When she licked her lower lip in a wanton gesture, I changed my plans.

"Get over here," I demanded. The confusion I expected lit her eyes. She scooted toward me until she sat on the edge. Grabbing my length in my hand, I began to stroke it as she watched. The heavy rise and fall of her tits and the look of blatant desire in her eyes told me everything I needed to know.

"You liked watching Cookie suck on Chains's cock. Is that because you liked watching or because you were imagining your lips wrapped around his cock?" I was intentionally crude.

"I—" she started but then stopped.

"Cat got your tongue?" I asked as I continued to slowly stroke. The glistening bead of precum at the end of my dick caught her attention, and I saw the tip of her pink tongue peek out to touch her lower lip again.

"You want to suck me, don't you?" I taunted in a soft voice as the shining liquid rolled over the head and down to my fingers.

She surprised me when she looked me straight in the eyes and nodded.

"Then what are you waiting for?" I released the grip I had on my cock, and it immediately bobbed in front of her.

Leaning forward, she gingerly wrapped her slender fingers around me.

"Tighter," I instructed, and she squeezed me with the perfect amount of pressure. Then she leaned further forward, and the tip of her tongue came out to lick the leaking head like a goddamn lollipop. When she flattened her tongue along the bottom and wrapped her lips around my girth, she elicited a groan out of me that came straight from the depths of my soul.

Sliding off the edge of the bed to her knees, she took me deeper.

As she became bolder, I fisted her hair and guided her speed and depth. On one particularly deep thrust, she gagged, and I nearly came on the spot. She recovered and slid her hand up closer so less of my cock went in her mouth.

"No. Let go and hold my hips," I demanded. Her eyes looked up at me in disbelief. I'd be a fucking liar if I said the sight of her on her knees with a mouthful of my dick, lips stretched around it, and shock in her kaleidoscope gaze, didn't make me want to shoot my load down her pretty little throat.

After a brief heartbeat, she did as I said, and her smooth hands held my hips. As I began to stroke in and out of her mouth, her fingers dug into my ass cheeks.

"Relax your throat and swallow when I hit the back," I said in a raspy tone. She did as she was told, and my eyes were damn near rolling back in my head at her compliance. She was an excellent pupil, and with each stroke into her warm and willing mouth, I was reeling.

"Enough," I finally ground out through clenched teeth. She had me on the verge of exploding as I pulled her off my cock by the handful of thick blonde hair I had fisted. As her lips released me with a pop that echoed through the quiet room, I raised her to her feet. "Get on the bed. Hands and knees, with your knees on the edge."

Without argument, she did as I instructed. Her compliance was a beautiful thing.

Gripping her ass, I reveled in the way her back arched. Pulling her open, I groaned at the glistening pussy bared to me. Unable to resist, I crouched behind her and ran my tongue through the slick folds of her plump wet lips.

Pausing after the first taste, I sighed. "Fucking nirvana," I said before diving back in.

Her mewls of pleasure and the way she thrust her core back to my greedy mouth drove me crazy. Lapping at the wetness of her excitement, I drove my tongue into her as I wanted to do with my aching cock.

"Jesus, Ogun. Oh my God," she gasped as I stepped up the pace. When I slipped two fingers inside her tight channel and curled them, that was all it took. Her juices flowed over my tongue like an elixir of the gods.

Not wasting a drop of it, I licked and sucked her until she shuddered and her face dropped to the bed. "Ogun," she murmured, and my inner beast wanted to roar.

One last taste, and I stood behind her. Gripping my cock, I lined it up with her now dripping hole. "I'm clean. You?"

"Last I checked, yes," she gasped.

"You on the pill?" I rasped. Though I never would've with anyone else, I needed to feel her raw.

"Uh-huh," she dazedly murmured.

"Thank fuck," I growled as I fed the tip in and then thrust hard. She jolted up off the bed with a cry. I knew I was big and she was probably burning as she stretched around me, but I could only give her a second to adjust because every fiber in my being screamed at me to fuck her.

When the tight lines of her back relaxed, I grabbed her hips and slid out nearly to the end before plunging balls deep into her glove-like sheath. "Perfect," I panted before repeating the motions.

With each stroke, her ass jiggled and made me want to fuck her harder. Looking up, I caught our refection in the mirror in front of me. Needing to see her expression, I reached up to wrap her wavy hair around my hand and pulled her head back.

"Open your eyes," I told her with a tug. Her pleasure-glazed gaze caught mine in the mirror. "Watch us."

Her lips parted with my next thrust. "Ogun," she gasped in surprise.

"I'm gonna fuck you so hard, you'll remember this night for the rest of your life," I told her as I pulled her back to whisper in her ear.

"Yes," she boldly agreed, holding my heated gaze in the mirror.

With a moan, I let loose and fucked her hard and fast. With each slide in and out, I could feel myself unraveling. She was more than I deserved, but the voracious beast within shattered through its cage, and I drove relentlessly into her tight cunt over and over.

"Oh, shit," she whimpered. "I'm going to come!"

"Yes," I grunted, and she exploded. Her pussy became unbelievably tight before it began to pulse around me. Needing to revel in the feel of it, I held myself within her hot, throbbing core.

Sweat dripped from my brow and ran down my chest.

It wasn't long before I couldn't contain myself any longer. Looking down to see the wetness coating every inch of where we were joined, I groaned. I began to move again. Watching my cum-slicked cock slide in and out of her swollen pink flesh was driving me mad.

I released her silky locks and pulled out.

"Lay on the bed." I needed to see her eyes in front of me when I filled her.

Without protest, she rolled over and moved up the bed. Lids heavy with lust, she reached up to hold the headboard and spread her tanned legs. Fuck, she was perfect.

Once she was settled, I crawled up between those open legs and buried myself in her with a single brutal thrust. My arms tensed, and the muscles strained as I held myself over her. Those perfect tits bounced, and she grunted along with me as I lost myself in her heaven.

Bracing on one hand, I cupped her full breast with the other hand. My thumb and forefinger plucked at her nipple as I leaned down and flicked the other with my tongue.

I couldn't get enough of her. I wanted to touch and taste every inch of her. I wanted to drown in her—lose myself within her. With precision, I bit her nipple, not enough to cause damage, but enough that she gasped and dug her nails into me.

Pulling back, I locked my eyes with hers as I made good on my promise to fuck the ever-loving hell out of her. With each movement, I lost a part of my soul to her.

That knowing tingle began at the base of my spine, and I groaned. "I'm going to fill this tight cunt with my cum, and you're going to come with me," I told her.

"I can't," she breathlessly argued.

"Bullshit. You're going to squeeze that perfect pussy around my cock to milk every fucking drop from me." It was a demand I knew she'd follow, because I could already feel her muscles tensing and her snug sheath swelling around my shaft. Her eyes were locked with mine as she took every stroke with a catch of her breath.

With the first pulse, she arched her back and screamed my name. It was all it took to make me lose it.

"Yes! God, yes! That's it, baby. Come all over me," I crooned as I shot jet after jet of hot cum all the way up against her cervix. With each burst, I shattered into a million pieces. It was unlike any other time in my life.

Without pulling out, I dropped to my elbows on either side of her. My lips pressed to the bounding pulse I could see in her neck. Needing more, I licked the salty sweat from her as I bit down on the tender skin where her neck met her shoulder. A final blissful shudder shot through me.

Her hands dropped down to my sweat-soaked hair, and she held me against her equally damp chest. It was as if she sensed this was no casual fuck. There was something deeper at work than either of us had anticipated. I'd never planned on having a woman that I claimed as my own.

At least not before the vision that had hit me like a ton of bricks at the restaurant.

It explained why I'd been fascinated with her from the first day I'd laid eyes on her in those cute scrubs.

The woman whose heart was pounding against my chest was destined to be mine.

After dozing off still buried in her heaven, I woke to her snugged into my side. Blinking away my confusion, the events of the last couple of hours slammed into me.

My arm reflexively tightened around her, and she moaned as she arched against my hip. Sensing the heat emanating from her perfect pussy, my cock lengthened and throbbed with need.

Gently rolling her over, I kneed her legs open and slid inside her slick, waiting sheath. The absolute sense of rightness settled in my soul as I watched her eyes flutter open and a sigh slip from her passion-swollen lips.

"Again?" she questioned, and I couldn't help the chuckle that escaped me.

"You complaining?" I asked before I pulled her nipple into my mouth and rolled my tongue around it. When I sucked it harder, she whimpered and arched closer.

If I fucked her fifty times a day, every day for the rest of my life, I didn't think it would be enough.

"You didn't use a condom," she hesitantly whispered.

Pulling away from her breasts, I stared into her hazel depths as I thrust into her hard enough to make her breath catch. "And I never will with you."

"What if I get pregnant?" she asked with a hint of fear in her eyes. "The pill isn't infallible. And how do I know you're clean just because you say you are?"

Where that would've terrified me in the past to the point that I'd actually doubled up condoms, with her I didn't care. The vision I'd had of her dressed in white and kissing me with a smile on her beautiful face told me she was… everything. I knew that regardless, she'd be mine, and one day, I hoped she'd carry my baby, too.

Imagining her soft belly swollen with my child actually made my cock swell.

The widening of her eyes told me she felt it.

"I'm not worried about that, and if you need them, I can give you lab results. I've never been bare with another woman," I murmured as I withdrew and slid forward again.

She wrapped her legs around me and gripped my shoulders with her nails. The pain drove me forward. I didn't last long, but I managed to wring two more orgasms out of her before I emptied into her tight pussy for the second time that night.

Once we were done, I got up and padded to the bathroom. After grabbing a washcloth and wetting it with warm water, I returned, cleaned her up, and silently helped her dress. Then I pulled my now wrinkled clothes back on.

Before leaving the cocoon of the room, I threaded my fingers through her hair in the back of her head and pulled her into a deep kiss. Reluctantly, I broke free of her intoxicating lips.

Then, I inhaled a fortifying breath and stepped back.

"Come on," I said as I took her hand in mine and led her out into the clubhouse. The party was still going strong when we stepped outside.

Ignoring the knowing looks we received after stepping out into the night, I wrapped an arm around her shoulders and stopped next to Ghost's group. They were still sitting in the chairs but had given up their drinks for a joint they were passing around.

Chains tried to hide his smirk at our freshly fucked appearances, but he finally gave up and shook his head with a wide grin. Taking a deep drag, he stared at me. He knew as well as I did that she'd been raptly watching him get sucked off and I'd fucked her with the thought of it in the back of both of our minds.

"Hmm, we thought maybe you'd left," Ghost said with a knowing grin.

"No, he just came," chuckled Angel like a prepubescent boy. Kira covered her face and groaned. I rolled my eyes and pulled her into my side and kissed the top of her head to tell her I had her.

"Forgive them, they have no manners," I said with a chuckle.

"Rumor has it we might've been raised by wolves," chortled Phoenix before he took a heavy toke and started coughing.

Chains took the joint from Phoenix as he rolled his eyes. Then he muttered, "Some of us could've been so lucky."

"Quit hogging it. Puff, puff, pass, asshole." Ghost jokingly backhanded Chains on the elbow. For doing so, he took a massive drag and blew the smoke in Ghost's face.

"You're such a dick," Ghost muttered. While Ghost was waving the smoke out of his face, Angel reached across the circle and took the joint from Chains and stuck it to his lips.

Ghost opened his eyes after waving wildly and saw Angel with the joint. "You all are a bunch of fucking assholes," he grumbled as he slouched back in his seat. Croc laughed and damn near tipped his chair over.

"Are they always this nice to each other?" Kira asked with an expression of uncertainty.

They all busted up laughing. "Yeah, babe. Pretty much," said Angel as he gave me a wink.

I took the empty seat that Squirrel had vacated and pulled Kira down into my lap. The guys all watched us with one eye as they continued to joke with each other. I knew they weren't missing a thing and were likely biding their time to give me shit.

I took a single drag from the joint that Angel passed me and blew the smoke away from Kira. Out of courtesy, I held it up in offering to Kira, but something told me she wouldn't take it.

"No, thank you," she politely declined. I decided to have

mercy on poor Ghost. Handing it on to him, I smirked as he gave a harrumph to the rest of my brothers.

We sat and bullshitted with everyone for a while. When I noticed she was starting to doze off, I figured I better get her home. Though I'd love to keep her with me all night, I didn't know if she was ready for that.

Fucking was one thing. Staying the night was a whole other level.

"Hey, sleepyhead," I murmured in her ear. She snuffled into my neck, and I had to fight the chub that wanted to pop. "Kira," I tried again.

"Why don't you just take her back to your room? You obviously wore her out." Angel snickered.

"Can't. Zaka is loose in the house because I didn't plan on being gone all night."

"Oh, shit. Yeah, that monster will eat your house in half if you don't go home," Angel said with wide eyes. Angel had been there the first time I came home after leaving Zaka out of his crate all night. It wasn't pretty.

"Well, you can leave her here with me," offered Chains with a grin.

"Fuck you," I said, though there was very little heat behind my words, since I knew he was only fucking with me.

"So is that serious?" Angel asked me with a straight face as he motioned toward the woman dozing in my lap.

Not wanting to admit what I'd seen and where my head was, I shrugged. Angel leaned forward with his elbows on his knees as he stared in my eyes.

"Don't lie to me," he said quietly. He and I had been friends since I moved in next door to him twenty-three years ago. We knew each other better than any of the other brothers.

"I don't want to talk about it yet," I admitted reluctantly. My gaze dropped to the dark golden head resting on my shoulder. Emotions heavier than I was ready for shot through me like a bolt of electricity.

"Well, that's at least honest," he said as he looked up through the dark hair that had fallen across his eyes. "If you want, my truck is out back. I can bring it around if you want to drive her home."

The thought of being cooped up in his truck, no matter how nice it was, sent a shudder of revulsion down my spine. I sighed. "Okay, fine. Thanks. I'll bring it back tomorrow morning."

"No rush. I have my bike," he said with a shrug.

He went to go pull his jet-black Dodge around and stopped on the driveway. He left it running and hopped out.

Standing, I tried not to jostle Kira, because I actually loved carrying her. Once I got close, he opened the passenger door, and I settled her in the seat. With her seat belt fastened and her mouth falling open, she continued to sleep. I chuckled and closed the door.

"You sure you know what you're doing?" he asked me.

Swallowing hard, I ran a hand through my hair. "Fuck, no," I said. Despite my gift, I had no idea what the future might hold other than the fact that Kira Baranov was mine.

SIX

Kira

"SEX ON FIRE"—KINGS OF LEON

My phone ringing woke me up, and I groaned. My hand thumped around on my nightstand for it. Finally coming into contact with it, I dragged it over to the bed.

"Hello?" I mumbled with the pillow over my eyes. I ached every-fucking-where. In the best of ways, but Ogun hadn't been lying when he said I'd never forget that night. He'd shown me how incredibly blah my sex life had been before him.

"Kira," the Russian-accented voice snapped.

I shot up to a sitting position so fast, my pillow fell to the floor. Sasha's head rose from the bed as if sensing danger.

"Father?" I hated how my voice wavered as I spoke. But he did that to me. No matter how accomplished I thought I'd become, he always had the ability to knock me back down to the little girl of my past.

"What the hell do you think you're doing?" His voice dripped disdain, but I honestly wasn't sure exactly what he was referring to. We hadn't been in contact for over a year.

Not since I'd refused to be his pawn and marry the man he'd chosen for me.

Except before that, he'd essentially disowned me when I ran off to Iowa to college. He'd been against me going to college as much as he hated the idea of me becoming a veterinarian. Hence the huge student loan debt I'd been saddled with.

"I have no idea what you're talking about," I replied. It shouldn't surprise me that he kept tabs on me despite our distance and lack of communication. Yet it did.

"Don't be stupid, Kira."

My fist clenched, and my heart ached. He always treated me as less than my brothers because I'd been born a girl. But the worst part was the verbal abuse I'd endured because of it. He'd called me stupid, worthless, a waste, vapid; you name it, if it was derogatory, he'd likely addressed me with it. Unless we were in public. Then I was his perfect little princess.

"Considering you haven't spoken to me in over a year, how would I possibly know what you're talking about?" I was proud of how I'd grabbed myself by my lady-balls and said what I wanted.

"You might want to remember who you're talking to, Kira." He spat my name out like it left a bad taste in his mouth. "I'm going to need you to think twice about who you're associating with. It's bad enough that you want to work with *animals*. But to be seen cavorting with a bunch of bikers, specifically those bikers of all people, is beyond reprehensible. Don't let me hear that you've been seen with them again. Unless you want me to make life very difficult for them. Do you hear me?" he demanded.

"Yes, I hear you," I said between clenched teeth. What I didn't say was that while I heard him, it didn't mean I was going to obey him. I was a grown-ass woman, for fuck's sake.

He didn't even bother saying goodbye. The call simply

ended. Sasha whimpered as she nuzzled her head against me. Absently, I petted her to tell her it was okay.

"Fucking asshole," I muttered. Then I wondered how he knew. Had he sent one of his damn minions to spy on me? Or was it one of my brothers? That hurt if it was, because I missed them and would've hoped if they were in town they would've at least said hello before tattling. Well, all of them except for Anatoly. He was the oldest and a prick. Worse than a prick. I hated him. Viktor and Dmitry I loved desperately.

Viktor was older than me, and Dmitry was younger. Dmitry was a professional hockey player like our cousin, Jericho.

Suddenly, my perfect life that I thought was mine and mine alone seemed so much more fragile.

Dropping my gaze to my phone, I realized I'd slept ridiculously late. I was surprised Sasha had let me sleep so long.

There was also a message from Ogun that actually made me smile.

Zaka's Dad: Hope you slept well

My heart thumped ridiculously hard upon reading his words. One date, and I'd hopped in the sack with him. Granted, in my defense, he'd been asking me out for months. It wasn't like I'd met him last week.

Biting my lip, I started having second thoughts about what I'd done. Not because he was in a motorcycle gang. No, a motorcycle *club*. Also, not because they smoked weed. Because I couldn't care less what people did as long as they didn't push it on me, which they didn't.

Glancing down at my phone, I fought an internal debate on whether to answer or call this all off. It really wasn't fair to dump all the shit that came with me on his doorstep.

Except, when I asked myself how I'd feel about seeing him

at his next appointment and knowing he might've moved on with someone else, the ache in my chest was my answer.

Before I could change my mind, I tapped out a reply.

Me: Like a rock

His reply was immediate, and it caused a silly smile to spread across my face.

Zaka's Dad: Interesting. Wonder why

Me: Gee I wonder

Zaka's Dad: You think you'll have trouble sleeping tonight?

It was impossible not to start giggling. Geneva must've been awake, because at the sound of my laughter, there was a knock at the door. Sasha jumped up and ran to the door with a bark. "Yeah?"

The door cracked open. "You decent?" she asked from the other side.

"Yes, you dork," I replied with another laugh. Sasha darted around her legs, and I heard the doggie door rattle as she rushed out into the backyard.

"Well, someone must've had a good time last night." Her smirk accompanied a waggling of her brows, and I threw my pillow at her as I tried not to give in to the schoolgirl giggles from earlier.

"Stop it," I said through the smile that escaped and my eye roll.

Knowing few boundaries, she plopped onto my bed and propped her chin in her hands. "Spill. You can't go out with someone that hot and that bad without sharing it."

"Says who?" I chuckled. My phone dinged again, and I read the next message.

Zaka's Dad: Is that a yes? No? Don't leave me hangin

Before I could type out a reply, Geneva grabbed my phone and rolled away.

"Give it back, you shit," I said and crawled toward her, scrambling to get at it. She played keep away with it as she read my messages.

"Oh my God! Tell me you played hide the salami with that sexy beast of a man. Please," her eyes were wide and excited. Hugging my phone to her chest, she batted her eyes.

I held my hand out.

"Not gonna kiss and tell," I said, then wiggled my fingers, demanding my phone. She shook her head.

"Uh-uh. Spill, Ki. Cuz something happened if you're saying you won't kiss and tell." She was biting her lip and almost jumping up and down with glee. I shook my head. "Tell me or I'm gonna tell him you need a repeat performance."

"You wouldn't," I said in warning.

"Fess up. I need the dirt." She gave me a cheesy, smug smile.

"No. Give me my phone," I said with narrowed eyes.

A devilish gleam flickered in her gaze and she started tapping on my phone as I squealed and darted toward her. She ran away from me, I chased her, she jumped up and ran across my bed as I crawled after her over the mattress.

"Sent!" she boasted, panting from our brief escapade.

Mouth hanging open, I tried like hell to keep from killing her. With a devious chuckle, she tossed my phone to my bed. I swooped it up and unlocked it, kicking myself for ever giving her my unlock code.

Me: I'm going to need a repeat. STAT. If not, I might not sleep for days

Zaka's Dad: Say no more

"Oh my God, Geneva! What the actual fuck?" I shouted.

Because though I'd answered his text, I knew I needed to chill with him until my father calmed down.

Me: Ogun wait.

He didn't answer. I sat on the edge of the bed and waited another few seconds.

Me: Ogun!

No answer. So I called.

It rang.

And rang.

"Maybe he's busy," I rationalized.

"Maybe he's on his way," she gloated.

"Shit." I jumped up and ran to the bathroom to shower. As the water heated up, I frantically brushed my teeth, finishing the job in the shower. With a cursory wash of my hair and body, a good wash of the lady bits, I ripped the shower curtain back and toweled off.

I'd barely wrapped the towel around my hair when I heard a bike pull up. "No." I ran to the window and peeked through the curtains in time to see a hint of sexy step onto the front porch and out of sight.

The doorbell rang as I was wrapping my second towel around me.

As I jerked open the closet to get clothes, my door opened and closed, and I spun around.

"Don't bother, you look perfect the way you are." He began stalking toward me. Ineffectively, I held out a hand, thinking it might actually ward him off.

"Ogun, wait. I didn't send the message," I tried to argue. The problem was, my body was betraying me. I wasn't wet between my legs from the shower.

He reached out, grabbed the front of my towel in his meaty

fist, and pulled me into his hard body. When his lips crashed into mine, I melted into him. Despite my initial resolve, my head angled to accommodate the fiery kiss. The movement caused my towel to unwrap from my head, and my wet hair cascaded down my back.

"Goddamn, you taste delicious," he murmured against my lips. The next thing I knew, my towel was on the floor, my back was against my closet door, I was kissing him like the world was ending, and he was unzipping his pants.

His thick fingers slid through my wet folds, and he groaned. The next breath had my legs wrapped around his waist and the entire massive length of his shaft buried in my core to the hilt. We both let out a raspy moan at the action.

Without batting an eye, he fucked me against that door with my arms over his shoulders, my hands clutching his hair and the soft leather of his vest. It was fast, rough, and incredibly wanton.

But I loved it.

Every thrust.

Every grunt.

Before I knew it, I was shamelessly screaming his name as he pulsed inside me with an animalistic groan.

"Fuck, babe."

"Oh my God," I said on a sigh.

"I missed you," he muttered against the side of my head. I breathlessly chuckled.

"It's only been like nine hours," I said as my legs tightened around his waist and my arms hugged his neck.

"Nine hours too long," he said as he gave a little thrust of his hips, causing me to shudder with an aftershock of pleasure.

"I really didn't send the message," I gasped with a final shiver that caused him to start slipping out. My legs tightened around him, and he chuckled.

"I really don't care," he said with a smirk. Carefully, he slipped loose of my body and set me on my feet. The hot, wet liquid running down the inside of my thighs gave me a terrifying realization.

"You didn't use a condom again!" I whisper-yelled.

"Told you I wasn't going to. I'll provide you with fucking lab results, what the fuck ever you need, but I ain't using a rubber with my woman. Fuck. That." My heart stuttered at his words.

"Ogun, about that… we need to talk." I bit my lip because it hurt to consider telling him what I was about to say, let alone actually spit the words out. To distract myself, I grabbed one towel to wrap back around my naked body.

His eyes narrowed suspiciously as he used the other towel to wipe himself off before tucking his thick length back in his pants. The slide of his zipper and the clink of his buckle almost made me whimper with disappointment.

"We can't do this again," I began, but he held up a hand. Nervously, I gripped the towel.

"You can stop right there. I don't care what your excuse is, I'm not having it. When I told you that you were my woman, did you think I was kidding?"

"I—"

"No. Let me answer my own question, because I can assure you, I wasn't. That's something a Royal Bastard doesn't fuck around with. Claiming an ol' lady is serious shit, Kira."

"Ogun—"

His hand spanned the front of my throat the way he seemed to like to do and pulled me close. He gave a light squeeze before pressing his lips to mine. This kiss was so far removed from the mutual assault of our previous kisses that it left me weak in the knees.

"You're mine, Kira." He nipped my bottom lip in a teasingly sultry way that sent my heart racing and my lungs shutting down. It was like an all-out war on my senses that had my body in overdrive.

"God, Ogun, you—" Another kiss shut me up.

"I have some shit to take care of, but I'll be back tonight. Pack a bag with enough for a couple of days. You're staying with me."

"But Sasha," I started. The sound of her name sent her sailing into the room and plowing into Ogun. Little traitor that she was, she was licking the hell out of his hands and arms.

"Bring her. I'll cage it over."

"Ogun, I can drive," I argued, then wondered what the hell I was thinking. Why the actual fuck was I going along with his bossy, asinine demands?

"I'll text you when I'm on my way," he said and then he was gone.

In frustration, I huffed. *How dare he order me around like I'm his property!*

"Damn you, Ogun Dupré!" I growled out. When he got back, I'd try to convince him that anything further happening between us was a really bad idea.

Looking down at where Sasha was staring curiously up at me, I shook my head.

"Don't you go and take his side. You hear me?"

Her answer was to tip her head in the opposite direction.

SEVEN

Voodoo

"REBEL"—SHALLOW SIDE

Some people say that what I practice is more hoodoo than voodoo. It's a blend of many beliefs. After all, voodoo isn't a uniform worship. It's a combination of multifaceted influences that each individual or group perceives in their own special way.

Because death is a regeneration of society as a whole in the voodoo culture, my grandmother's family has held heavy belief that those souls that are truly evil need to be prevented from passing on into the next life. That's the only way to keep them from returning to the earth again to rain terror and evil on society again. Therefore, it's my job to ensure that the proper rituals have been performed to allow for either safe passage or none at all.

As I knelt at the table that served as my altar in the shed that served as my temple behind the hog farm our chapter owned, I carefully laid the tarot cards out on the table one b one. Studying them carefully, I continued to softly sing one of the songs I'd been taught at a young age by my mother and waited for the answers I sought.

The candles flickered softly, and I knew I was likely not alone. Without fear, I chanted the words that were like breathing to me.

It was different for each of us in my family with the gift. For me, if I was actively seeking answers, I needed to enter a near trancelike state. My eyes remained fixed on the story the cards told as the lines and colors blurred.

It was then that the *loas* spoke and I knew what my course of action would be. Breathing deeply of the burning herbs, I returned my *gris-gris* to their proper places, painted my face, closed the ceremony, and rose to my feet. Before I stepped outside, I remembered to grab my phone.

It vibrated in my pocket for the twentieth time, and I cursed. It had been ringing when I went into my sanctuary, but I'd silenced it and set it to the side, knowing I'd call whoever it was back.

Ordinarily, I would've let the call go to voicemail again, because I had a job to do. Except something told me to check it, and I never ignored my instincts. When I saw who it was, I smiled.

"Granmé," I said warmly as I paused with my hand on the doorknob.

"Ogun. You are safe?" Her tone was hurried and fearful.

"Of course," I replied as if it was crazy for me to be anything but.

"Your father's people were here," she whispered. She never referred to Hawk as my father. He was my dad or my papa. My father was the man whose evil blood unfortunately tainted my heart.

"Are you okay?" My first concern was her safety. She'd been an important part of my life until I was six years old. Then she'd come to visit us as often as she could as I was growing up, but I'd talked to her on the phone almost every day.

"I'm fine. Your papa and Jameson were here, thankfully. But you must listen to me. Your father is alive. They said he's going after you." Her hurried, gasping breaths worried me.

"What the hell? Granmé? What's wrong?"

"Just a flesh wound. Thanks to my boys," she said, and I heard my mother's voice in the background.

"Let me talk to my mother," I demanded. There was a whisking and rustling sound, and my mother came on the line.

"Ogun. She's telling the truth. She's okay. Hurt—but okay. We had gone into town, and Jameson offered to escort us back because Mother had her vision again of being attacked. She tried to play it off as nothing—"

"It was nothing! I'm alive, as you can see! I told you it wasn't my time!" I heard Granmé grumble in the background.

"Mother! Enough! Ogun, listen. She not only saw herself being attacked, she also saw your father kill you. Now today, she was attacked, and the men said…." My mother sounded worried and confused. Then again, so was I.

"My father is dead," I insisted.

"That's what we thought. But what if he isn't? Ogun—promise me you will be careful. We're coming home early. Hawk wants to be there to help protect you." The last was said quietly and tearfully.

"No. Granmé needs you there. I'll be careful, and I'll tell the brothers. We'll stay vigilant, but it's unlikely that he's alive, and if he is, it's doubtful he knows where I am. It's been over twenty-two years with no word from him," I rationalized.

"I don't know, Ogun. I think she might be right. After all, you didn't hear from your father initially because the club made him believe we had died. Then we thought he was dead. Please, baby, be careful." My mother only called me *baby* when she was emotional. Which was exactly what I chalked it up to then—high emotions related to her mother's injuries.

"Is Papa nearby?" I asked, because I needed other answers.

"Yes. Hold on. I love you, Ogun," she said, then handed the phone off to Hawk.

"Son, everything okay up there?" His gruff voice carried over the line.

"Yes. I'm in the middle of something though. The men that attacked Granmé—did you see them?"

He snorted. "Sure did."

"And were they from Gambler's club?" I didn't want to say their name. Simply thinking it made my lip curl in distaste.

"Oh yeah," he replied.

"How can you be sure?"

"Because the dumb fuckers were wearing their cuts."

I swore under my breath. "Where are they now?"

"Gator bait." He chuckled. "And the bikes they left by the landing like morons are deep in the swamps." Relief lifted a load of worry off my shoulders. If they were dinner for the gators, they obviously wouldn't be running back to their club to tell tales.

"Do you think they were telling the truth? About Gambler?"

"Son, I don't know. Your grandfather said he'd been taken care of, so I don't have a good answer for that." Frustration laced his voice.

"Where the hell would he have been for the last twenty-some years?"

"Don't know that either. Jameson hasn't been back all that

long, but he's got his boys looking into it too. Hold on, he wants to talk to you." There was some rustling before I heard Jameson's voice on the line.

"Voodoo, brother, I'm sorry this shit happened. If we'd known any of this was going to happen, we would've had someone out here to keep an eye on her."

I scoffed. "Don't feel bad, she wouldn't have allowed it. Stubborn woman," I grumbled.

He snorted. "She might be stubborn, but she's fierce. I just wish we could get her to realize she's not immortal."

I heard my grandmother shout in the background, "*Beau diable!* You quit telling tales! You don't know. Maybe I shall live forever!"

Her outburst had me shaking my head with a wry grin. "Ask Hawk to keep Mama and Granmé safe. I need to finish up with work. The boys are waiting on me."

The huffed sigh that he let loose was followed with, "You know I will, and I'll also put a prospect out here in the swamps too. Get to work—you're not getting paid to stand around talking on the phone. Hawk and I will call Venom and fill him in on what happened down here."

"Roger that," I said with a smile. "Thanks, bro."

The waning sun told me I'd been in the temple longer than I realized. It often happened, but that day, I had a job to do and someplace to be afterward.

Cutting through the trees that concealed my temple, I emerged on the other side of the main farm site. An odd feeling of being watched hit me, and I scanned my surroundings. Nothing out of the ordinary seemed to be moving. It wasn't the first time I'd experienced that. Reminding myself to read my cards, I approached the slaughterhouse.

"Voodoo, you ready?" Squirrel asked as he leaned on the outside of the building. His head cocked to the side and down, he watched me through raised eyes as he inhaled deeply from the joint held to his lips.

I nodded and stepped inside the slaughterhouse with Squirrel on my heels. Phoenix and Blade were waiting for us.

"I still don't understand that weird-ass shit you do," Squirrel murmured, and I narrowed my eyes at him.

"You have room to talk," I replied.

"Chill, bro. Didn't mean nuthin' by it."

I was used to people not having a grasp on my beliefs and abilities, which was why I kept those abilities to myself unless I was with those I trusted. Squirrel, I trusted, or I'd have never voted him in as a brother, but he had a habit of getting on my nerves.

"Let's get this over with. Venom called church for that De Luca job," Ghost said as he came out of the shadows.

"Jesus fucking Christ, Ghost. Stop that shit," Phoenix muttered as he ran a hand over his face. Ghost chuckled as he shrugged unapologetically.

Stepping up to the battered man staked spread eagle on the floor, I tried to find a shred of compassion for his human life, but I couldn't. He was the worst kind of scum. We'd been paid extra to make him suffer. Every sick thing he'd done to the children he'd messed with was to be done to him—and then some.

Taking in the giant dildo shoved up his ass, I raised a brow to Ghost, who shrugged. "Seemed only fair. I sure as shit wasn't sticking *my* dick up there."

Despite the situation, I snickered.

"Who are you?" he asked with scared, wide eyes as I pulled on a pair of nitrile gloves. He should be frightened.

Not saying a word to him, I crouched and proceeded to draw a series of symbols on his naked skin using the tip of a razor-sharp silver knife. The first cut was such a shock that he didn't make a peep. By the second, he shrieked like a little girl. It fed the beast that was stirring within me. Ripples of darkness ran through me as it fought to come to the surface. Shoving it back, I maintained my focus. This wasn't the time to let it free.

Once I had control, I mirrored the symbols in pig's blood.

He became increasingly agitated, screaming and struggling against the chains that held him in place. By that time he was shrieking at me. I ignored his pleas that turned to threats until he mentioned something I wasn't expecting.

"What did you just say?" I asked as I paused. The brothers in the room with me stepped closer, telling me they'd heard what I heard.

"I said you're going to regret this, because the Scorpions are going to be coming for you," he said, obviously feeling like that had given him power.

My eyes flashed to Facet. It was his job to find out every detail of the person's life before we brought them here. He shook his head with a frown. He hadn't found a connection between this piece of shit and the Scorpions.

"I don't believe you," I said as I continued with my job. He screamed again. As if anyone would hear him.

"Mule is my cousin," the man rapidly threw out. I again looked to Facet, who appeared disbelieving and still shook his head. Mule was the vice president of the Scorpions down in south Des Moines. He was also a real piece of shit, so it wouldn't surprise me if there was a relation between them.

"Funny, we never found that information anywhere," Phoenix said from his position over by Facet.

"That's because he was adopted. It was a closed adoption, we only found each other recently. You kill me, and he'll be gunning for you." The man thought he actually had bargaining power, and I found that humorous.

"And you think that scares us?" Ghost asked with a deadly calm.

"Come on, I have a wife and kids," he pleaded. That was knowledge we did have, and it curdled my stomach to think about. Especially because we knew his own children had suffered at his hands.

"Maybe you should have thought about how much they supposedly meant to you before you destroyed any chance they had at a normal life," Blade said from the chair he sat in as he organized his tools on the rolling cart.

Blade was a fucked-up individual. Then again, with the life he'd had, it probably shouldn't be a surprise.

"Oh. You won't be needing this anymore," I said as I used the scalpel-like knife to slice off his flaccid penis. That was one of the specific requirements of this particular job.

That got his attention. He began screaming at the top of his lungs—eyes wild.

"You're all dead! You hear me? You're all fucking dead!" he screamed at us with spittle flying. At least until I shoved his spongy cock down his sick, twisted throat. Like a cold, calculating machine, I stared him in the eye as he gagged. Then, I slid the blade up his abdomen to his neck. With surgical precision, I sliced along his carotid. First, one side, then the other. Then across his throat in a garish smile.

Bright crimson pooled around him as he tried to speak but couldn't. While the savage beast gnashed its teeth in the depths of my darkened soul, I continued to watch the life leave his eyes.

Once I was finished, I stood, peeled off the nitrile gloves, and told Blade, "I'm done. Finish up."

Ghost, Phoenix, Facet, and I stepped out to leave Blade to work his sick twisted magic on the guy.

Once Blade was done with him, he'd be fed to the hogs on the farm, and no one would ever find his body. It was one of the perks of owning a hog farm and came in handy with the disposal side of our business.

Hawk had inherited the farm from an uncle he'd barely known. The uncle didn't have any kids, so as his only living relative, he'd left it to Hawk. That had been years ago. At first he was going to sell it, because he said he didn't know the first thing about running a hog farm.

Then they had found out that hogs will eat any fucking thing. Especially the gigantic wild boars we bred there for hunting ranches. They were some ruthlessly savage creatures.

"You heading straight to the clubhouse?" Squirrel asked as he pulled his helmet on.

"Yeah," I said as I did the same, uncaring if I smeared the paint. It was cooler that day, thank fuck, because anytime we had business like that at the farm, we wore helmets. Less of a chance that someone would be able to point one of us out specifically. Then again, the local law enforcement didn't fuck with us too much. We paid them enough.

I flipped down the tinted visor and started up my bike. We all pulled out of the farm without a backward glance.

Coy and the boys down in our Louisville Chapter had a similar operation, but theirs was disguised as a Pet Crematorium and Funeral Services business. Crazy thing was, they actually did that shit too. People paid a lot of money to keep old Rover's ashes with them for all eternity.

The other thing we were in agreement with was their stance on the drug trade. Well, mostly. We made a lot of fucking money by transporting weed from Colorado to Iowa and down to Florida. False bottoms and a false wall in the front in the livestock trailers of the semis made for the perfect storage system. We made money from the hogs and the weed. It's the perfect cover.

But the harder shit? Fuck that. That shit was toxic to people, families, and society in general.

It didn't take long to reach the clubhouse, since it was down the road but on the same property as the hog farm, and we all backed in against the building. Though the temps were cooler, I was still sweating by the time we reached the clubhouse.

"Fucking hate those things," I bitched as I hung the helmet on the handlebar to let the sweat dry.

Phoenix chuckled. "Pussy," he teased. He wore one all the time, no exceptions. Then again, the fucker loved the heat because he barely felt it. If it wasn't for his special talents, he'd probably be down with a chapter in Texas. But we all had our reasons for being where we were.

"Fuck off," I said with a huff of laughter.

"You look scarier now than you did before," Squirrel muttered.

I flipped him off.

We stepped into the cool interior, and I left the guys at the bar to go back to Venom's office. Facet followed me but went into his room as I continued on. I already knew he was going to dig into what the guy had said about Mule.

Venom looked up as I knocked on the open frame. "Hawk called me. You okay?"

I nodded. Though I was worried about my grandmother, if my parents said she'd be okay, I believed them.

"It done?" He didn't need to elaborate; I knew he was asking about the job.

"Blade's working on the cleanup, but yeah." He nodded in satisfaction.

"Where's Raptor?" I asked as I sat down in the chair opposite the desk from him.

"Making the rounds with Kicker to check on the dry cleaning shop, the restaurants, and car washes." Also legit businesses that were perfect fronts for cleaning the dirty money we brought in.

"I wanted to let you know something that the guy at the farm said today," I started. He leaned back in his chair with an intense look.

"Does this need to wait for church?"

"I definitely plan to bring it up, but I wanted you to know first."

He nodded, and I told him about what the guy had said and about how I'd been feeling like I was being watched. He didn't like it either.

Once business was out of the way, we sat and shot the shit for a bit before he looked at the time. "Unless you wanna be cleaning shitters this weekend, I suggest we get to the chapel."

"Um, yeah, no thanks. Give me a minute to wash my face," I said as I stood and followed him out of the room. Once I'd washed the makeup off, I headed down the hall to the chapel at the end. We dropped our phones in the basket outside the room as we stepped in.

As always, the old-timers were there first. Goob, Shorty, E, and Break had pretty much all retired, so they hung out all day at the clubhouse to get peace from their ol' ladies. Well, except Shorty. He'd never gotten serious with anyone and swore he was a confirmed bachelor.

Kicker, Shank, Phoenix, Squirrel, Croc, and Ghost were at the table, too. Facet walked in after us with his laptop. It was the only electronic device ever allowed in church, because that thing had the highest security I'd ever seen. Encryption upon encryption and whatever other shit he had on it to protect the dealings he did for us on the dark web. It was where our jobs came in from. Most of the people we worked for didn't know who we were, and we didn't know them.

The guy in the slaughterhouse today was one of the few jobs we did where we had met the client who hired us in person. The woman had a lot of money and was willing to pay heftily for what had been done to her nephew. She'd even stood in the shadows for the first of the job today. Weird, but whatever.

"Oh, good. Thought I was gonna be last in again today," said Angel as he hurried in the door behind Raptor. Ghost laughed. The only ones who were exempt from cleaning shitters were the old timers, P and VP. Of course, Blade because he was occupied, but Venom would fill him in.

The pounding of boots across the floor was followed by Chains rushing in and looking around before he dropped his head. "Fuck," he muttered as everyone busted a gut.

"All right, Chains, shut the door. Everyone listen up. We got the information regarding the De Luca job. Once we go over the details, we'll vote as to whether we want to take the job. Blade already gave me the okay to vote for him by proxy." Venom motioned for Facet to continue with the info he'd received from Lorenzo De Luca.

Facet cleared his throat. "First of all, I found the info about that guy and Mule." He then went on to elaborate and let the rest of the brothers in on what the guy had said earlier. Turned out it was legit. None of us was overly worried, because the Scorpions would never be able to tie Mule's cousin to us.

Except I didn't like that they kept popping up in shit for us. That was twice in one day. I didn't like it.

Then he tapped away at his computer and opened the file he'd received from De Luca.

"Okay. So evidently Grishka Kalashnik killed his youngest son, Francesco."

"He knows that for sure?" Venom asked in surprise. While we might've known it wasn't an accident, to hear Kalashnik had been that ballsy was unnerving.

"According to this, he says Grishka boasted about it in a video that someone secretly recorded." Facet said.

"Someone as in who?" asked Raptor.

"One of his own men," said Facet as he looked up at all of us.

"Oh, shit," murmured several brothers. The dude was as good as dead if Kalashnik found out. And he would. If we'd seen it, and De Luca had seen it, then it was likely others had too.

"Okay, so we know he wants retaliation. What exactly does he want?" Venom asked.

"Cleanup and disposal of a certain daughter of the head of the Bratva in Chicago."

"Shit," mumbled Angel as he slouched in his chair. He hated when the job included women. In fact, we usually refused those jobs unless the woman was an absolute evil cunt.

"Shit is right," said Facet as his face went pale. His eyes met mine, and he slowly spun the computer around.

The room went silent as I stared at the beautiful, smiling face of my woman. Except instead of Kira Baranov, it said Kira Kalashnik. Heart pounding, I swore to fucking Christ the room started spinning. A vision of Kira in my arms with vacant eyes and covered in crimson flooded my senses, rocking me to my core. It was so real, I could smell the scent of her blood—taste its copper tang.

"No!" My fingers gripped the edge of the table as I shouted, and shit went flying off the walls. The few empty chairs fell backwards. Facet grabbed his computer and held it to his chest like it was a baby.

"Goddammit, Voodoo!" Venom shouted. His shouts barely penetrated my rage.

I was tackled out of my chair by Angel. His touch and Venom's began to calm me, and I found myself lying on the floor trying to catch my breath with huge, heaving gasps. Every fiber of my being was electrified and on edge.

"Voodoo, brother, listen to me. We're not taking the job, but I need you to think clearly. Calm your shit," Venom demanded.

Finally able to make my head and body cooperate, I swallowed hard and nodded. "Let me up," I whispered.

Angel and Venom both gave me hesitant looks but let go of me. We all got up, and I clenched my jaw as I took a deep, cleansing breath. "I'm good," I said.

"Look, I understand your reaction, but you gotta keep that shit under control," Venom said in a low tone. I nodded.

Once we were all back at the table, everyone turned serious eyes in my direction.

"This is my concern," Venom began. "If we don't take the job, De Luca may just find someone who will."

"Why her? Why not his oldest son? The one he's closest to," said Shank. Surprised that he knew so much about Kalashnik, I studied him with narrowed eyes.

"How do you know about them?" Raptor asked.

Shank snorted. "How do you think? I was in prison with one of his thugs. I heard things."

"That was years ago," said Raptor.

"So? You think he's not still up that boy's ass? Look him up," said Shank, causing Facet to open his computer again and start typing.

"He's right," said Facet as he scrolled, then looked at us. "Every picture of him shows his oldest son with him. Like, I wonder if he takes a shit with him in the room."

"Then you contact De Luca. You tell him she's my ol' lady and no one touches her. Tell him I'll take out the son myself," I growled.

"Voodoo. Think about this. How is she gonna feel about you killing her brother?" Angel said with concern. "I'll do it."

"Now, everyone hold on. We're not doing a motherfucking thing without putting it to the vote." Venom sounded exasperated and banged his fist on the table.

"We can't risk De Luca taking this job somewhere else," Angel firmly said. "You said so yourself."

"I know what I said, but that didn't mean we fly off the handle and start making plans that might rain hell down on this chapter or the entire club. Kalashnik has a lot of influence in a lot of places. De Luca is just as bad. Though he may be retired, he's still a powerful man." Venom was trying to reason with us, but there wasn't really any reasoning with me.

Holding his gaze, I said in a calm but deadly voice, "If I have to, I'll kill both De Luca and Kalashnik, but my woman is not getting harmed."

"Brother, you need to back the fuck up. You're talking some crazy-ass shit, now," Ghost said from the other side of the table. Croc was sitting next to him with his hands covering his face as he muttered to himself.

"First, Voodoo, is she your ol' lady? Because I didn't hear

you announce that before. Bringing her to a club party is a far cry from her being an ol' lady. She willing to do that? Tat and all?" Venom seemed to be staring into my soul, and I fought fidgeting.

Because the conversation she'd tried to start with me that morning about it not being a good idea for us to continue what we'd started slammed into my head. Except I'd had no idea she didn't just have skeletons in her closet—she had the whole fucking cemetery.

"I'll make sure she is," I said with finality.

EIGHT

Kira

"SELL MY SOUL"—SEETHER

"What am I going to do?" I asked as my shoulders slumped. Sasha tipped her head and looked at me questioningly. Then her big tongue lolled out of the side of her mouth and her tail thumped. I shook my head. "You're no help."

When I fell back on the bed, she bounded up and began to excitedly lick me. Despite my worry mere seconds ago, she had me laughing.

"Well, that's a far cry from the noises I heard coming from in here earlier," Geneva said from the open doorway. Sasha immediately paused and turned toward Geneva. She jumped down from the bed and began racing around like a lunatic.

"Sasha! Settle." At my command, she paused and sat, but I could sense the energy vibrating through her. "Outside, Sasha."

She took off like a shot, and I heard the doggie door flapping wildly.

"Sweet Jesus, that dog has energy!" Laughter bubbled out of my roommate.

"Don't I know it," I said as I realized that was another bad idea for me to go stay at Ogun's. What if Sasha's puppy exuberance hurt either Zaka or herself if she pissed Zaka off? He'd tear her to pieces.

"What's eating at you? You're not acting like a woman who got a wall-banging orgasm less than an hour ago," Geneva said with a shit-eating grin. My face flamed.

"Oh, Jesus," I muttered.

"Hey, there's no shame in having a man that can make you scream his name in under two minutes. Hell, I think I was screaming his name just from listening to you two." Her smile was pure devilment as she sat on my bed and leaned up against the headboard. "So what's the issue?"

Hesitating for a moment, I gazed at the ceiling fan as my shoulders slouched.

"He wants me to stay at his house for a couple of days," I finally admitted. She didn't reply, so I glanced her way. She was staring at me, blinking. I motioned for her to say something.

"I'm sorry. I was waiting for you to tell me what the problem was," she said with false confusion. I smacked her with one of my pillows.

"It's not that easy," I argued as she laughed.

Her expression sobered. "Kira. Before this Voodoo guy—"

"Ogun," I corrected.

"His cut said Voodoo, therefore I'm totally calling him that. Anyway, as I was saying before I was so rudely interrupted, before *Voodoo*, when was the last time you went out on a date?" She crossed her arms, waiting.

"I'm not sure. A few months ago?" I said, truthfully unsure.

"Months," she whispered to herself, rolling her eyes. "And how long has it been since you had a customer stop into the pink taco?"

"Oh, for fuck's sake!" I said as my face heated again.

"Answer the question," she said, then pursed her lips.

"Uhh." I was thinking, embarrassed to say that I thought it was halfway through vet school.

"If you have to think about it, it's been too fucking long. I get that vet school was challenging, but you need to have time for you. If all you ever have is your career, you're going to end up as a crazy cat lady. I'll be watching you on that show where people hoard animals, thinking, I knew her when she was young and normal." She'd leaned forward to speak earnestly, and I swatted her with the pillow again.

"I will not!"

She didn't answer. Instead, she raised her brows at me and said more with her look than she ever could with words.

"Geneva... it's complicated," I began. Chewing on my lip, I tried to figure out how to explain it.

"If it's your dad, he doesn't need to know that his little princess is banging a dirty biker down here in podunk Iowa." She was the only one who knew about my family. We'd spent the first four years of undergrad together, and she'd actually gone home with me for a couple of holidays.

Of course, my dad had been on his best behavior for her. Well, as good as he got, anyway.

"He already knows." I swallowed hard, feeling like a baseball was lodged in my throat.

"Oh, shit."

"Yeah. And he told me in no uncertain terms that I was to cease and desist any and all involvement with one sexy biker. Okay, so he didn't say it exactly like that." It was much worse.

"What the hell? How would he know that? Is he in town?" she asked in surprise.

"No. Which means he has someone watching me," I murmured and nervously picked at lint on my leggings.

"And that's not creepy at all," Geneva said in a voice heavy with sarcasm. "What the hell, Ki? Why would he do that? You're a grown-ass woman. You can do what you want and who you want."

She clearly didn't understand the Russian Bratva. Then again, she had no idea that was who my family was.

"My father is angry because he wanted me to marry someone and I refused." It was better not to get into too many details, because the life my family led was akin to something out of the movies. Most people had no idea things like that happened in real life.

"Ki, that's crazy. We don't live in the middle ages. Regardless of his beliefs, that doesn't give him the right to have you followed and then to threaten you." Disbelief had her voice rising to a near shriek. She was shaking her head, causing her red curls to bounce and fall in her face.

"My family is very old-school. My father immigrated to the US when he was a small boy. My mother was born here, but her parents were Russian born. They live by antiquated traditions. I'm not saying it's right, but it's what they know." It pained me to make excuses for my father, but I also didn't want to come out and say, "Yeah, my dad wants to me to marry the heir to the New York City Bratva to allow for a stronger alliance between the two."

"What about your mother? Is she okay with this?" Geneva asked in outrage. It almost had me smiling that she was championing me the way she was.

"No, but there isn't much she can do," I said with a sigh. My mother had been loved by her family, and they thought they were doing her a favor and honor by marrying her to my father. He had money; they had the elite bloodlines but no money. They had no idea the kind of man my father was.

"So my question to you is… what are you going to do?" Geneva asked as she gave me a worried glance.

"For now, I'm going to go switch my laundry." I shot her a half-hearted smile and got up from the bed.

"You know that's not what I was talking about."

"Yeah, but I don't want to think about it right now." Not waiting to see if she had more to say, I left the room and went to the laundry room. As I pulled my third load of laundry for the day from the wash and tossed it in the dryer, I heard Sasha barking, then the doggie door rattled and flapped.

Good Lord, she was going to rip it off one of these days.

The sound of voices registered over the sound of the dryer. Ass in the air as I sorted through the last of my clothes, I ignored whatever Geneva was up to.

"Now that's one of the best views I've had all day."

At the deep purr of Ogun's voice, I abruptly stood upright and spun around. "Ogun!"

The intensity of his stare was sending my heart rate into overdrive.

"What are you doing here so early?" I glanced at my watch to see that it was actually much later than I'd realized.

Sasha was desperately trying to shove her face into his hand for his attention. The chuckle that rumbled out of him did crazy things to me. Studying his interaction with my huge puppy, I again appreciated his masculine beauty. The thought of not seeing him again sucked.

Those icy-blue eyes met mine. "You got that bag packed?"

"Ogun… I told you I didn't think it was going to be a good idea."

"And I told you it was." His voice dropped down a notch.

"Besides, I need to talk to you about a few things. Are you sure you want your roommate to hear them?"

Suspicion making my brow furrow, I gave him a side-eye. "What kind of things?"

For the longest time, he simply stared at me. It was unnerving and I began to fidget.

"How about the fact that Grishka Kalashnik is your dear old dad?"

I froze.

"How did you know that?"

"How I know isn't as important as what I know. Now, unless you want to continue to discuss this here, I suggest you pack a bag." His expression gave nothing away.

My nervousness about what he knew or which side he was on was less than the worry I had about pulling Geneva into my hot mess. Surely, if he was telling me to pack a bag, he didn't intend to kill me. But what if he was supposed to take me to my father, or worse, Ivan?

It would be doubtful that my father would stoop to hiring Ogun's club if he held such disdain for them. Yet, with my father, one never knew. He wasn't above stooping to deplorable levels if it meant he got what he wanted. So using a club he looked down on wasn't a long shot.

"Did my father hire you?" I asked in a whisper.

"No."

Studying his eyes, I couldn't see signs that he was lying, but he could be good at it too. Except, something in my guts said he wasn't a liar.

"Okay."

It might be something I wouldn't live to regret, but I decided to trust him.

NINE

Voodoo

"TOPLESS"—BREAKING BENJAMIN

She quietly packed a bag. I was leaning against her dresser as she opened a drawer to get some underwear out. When she grabbed several conservative pairs, I glanced down and saw a few lacy numbers that she'd shuffled past. Picking them up, I held them out. "Pack these."

"What? You can't be serious." She looked at me like I had a dick on my forehead.

"I most certainly can."

Though she looked like she wanted to argue, she shot me a glare and shoved them in the bag she was packing. Once it was stuffed full, she paused.

"Am I still going to be able to take Sasha?" Worry flickered in her eyes but was quickly neutralized. Hearing her name, the naughty puppy ran at Kira and jumped up to shove her head in-between us.

"Why wouldn't you be able to take your dog?" I asked in

confusion. "Sit!" I told the dog and was pleased when she immediately obeyed.

"Because I don't know where you're taking me now, so I didn't know if the option was still there to take her," she replied with a slight quiver to her lower lip.

Realizing where her fear and worry was coming from, I had to set her mind at ease. "Relax, babe. We're still going to my place. Pack whatever you need for her for a few days." Honestly, I wanted to tell her to pack everything she owned because I didn't ever want her to leave. But I thought that might freak her out a little.

The tenseness left her shoulders, and she seemed to chill out. She walked out of the room to the kitchen where she filled a giant plastic zipper bag with about five or six scoops of dog food. Then she bent over to pick up the dog bowls, and I damn near had to bite my fist at the sight of her perfect ass in the air again.

The entire time, Sasha trailed behind her. If she could talk, I knew she'd be asking why Mom was taking her bowls away. Kira stopped. "Can you occupy her?"

I cocked my head in confusion. She silently tapped on a bag of dog treats. Understanding dawning, I called the big puppy as I walked to her room. "Come, Sasha!"

She raced after me and happily bounced around at my feet once I got there.

Kira walked in carrying a shopping bag that I assumed had all of Sasha's things.

"Ready?" I asked. She nodded and swallowed nervously. Maybe I should've put an end to her worry, but I didn't want to discuss shit in front of her roommate.

She led Sasha out to my Jeep and I helped her hook Sasha up to the harness rig I had for Zaka. I'd moved it to the back seat so Kira could ride up front, but I wasn't sure how Sasha would react to it.

I needn't have worried, because she was simply happy to be going for a ride.

We arrived at my house without a lot of discussion. Likely because we both had a lot on our minds. Also because the wind didn't allow for a lot of conversation without yelling.

Once we pulled into my garage, she faced me. "Tell me what's going on. I can't take this."

"Let's get inside and we'll talk." I reached up to push the button to close the garage door. Sasha was whining quietly in the back seat. Now that we'd stopped, her patience with the harness was running low. She'd need to get used to it, because she and Kira would be going places with me and Zaka.

At least, after we got the shit straightened out with her father. That had me wondering how I was going to tell her I'd agreed to kill her father or brother in place of her. Maybe she never needed to know that part.

Hell, I didn't know if De Luca would go for that idea anyway. Then I might have a real shitshow on my hands.

Once inside, I had to deal with the chaos that was Zaka in his crate. I'd kenneled him up when I left because I knew Sasha would be coming back with us. It would be better to reintroduce them in a controlled manner.

"Hold on to her. We'll take them into the backyard," I said as I handed Kira her dog's leash.

"Easy, boy. Settle," I told him as he damn near shook the kennel apart. He immediately sat and impatiently waited. I opened the door, slipped the harness on him, and clipped the leash to it. "Zaka, heel. Outside."

He followed me obediently out the back door. Kira followed

at a distance, but I knew Zaka had spotted them the second I let him out. He'd probably smelled them on me and was already cataloging them in his mind. He adored Kira.

"Sit," I told him. He followed my directions like a champ, and I was pretty sure it was because he was showing off for the ladies. I rolled my eyes, and a half-smile lifted my lips.

"Bring her over," I said softly to Kira, speaking in calm tones. She brought Sasha closer, and I could feel Zaka quivering in anticipation. He was fairly social when it came to other dogs, but you never knew.

"Easy," I said to him as he sniffed at Sasha. She jumped and darted to the side, but Kira got after her and kept a firm hand on her.

After a bit of letting them check each other out, I could sense they'd be okay. We gave them a loose leash first and they started to play. When there were no aggressive moves by either, we let them off the leash.

Kira laughed as they darted back and forth. They each had a turn tackling the other. Then Zaka showed her where the outdoor waterer was. They sloppily drank from the stainless steel basin I'd mounted under the spigot on my back patio.

"I think they'll be okay to play," I said and motioned for Kira to go inside.

After we got inside, I slid the inner door over the dog door so they wouldn't come flying in here to play and tear the house apart. Kira had taken a seat on one of the stools at my breakfast bar.

Knowing we needed to talk first, I told my surging dick to behave.

Unable to sit still due to the tension shifting through me, I paced. Finally, I decided it was probably like a Band-Aid—just rip it off.

"There's no easy way to say this, Kira. You have a hit out on you." I watched her closely to gauge her reaction.

Instead of the shocked look I expected, her entire body began to tremble. Not saying a word, she simply stared at me.

"Kira? Did you hear me?" I asked with narrowed eyes.

When her hazel eyes blinked, she inhaled shakily and exhaled on a rush. "Who?"

The fact that she didn't start freaking out about what I'd told her was proof that she likely knew more about her father than I'd expected.

"At the moment that doesn't matter," I began, but she cut me off.

"You can't just tell me that there's a hit out on me like we're discussing the chance of rain, then tell me it doesn't matter who ordered it," she snapped. Fuck, she was sexy when she was angry.

"Yes, I fucking can, because I have a way to fix it." At my words, she instantly looked suspicious.

"How?"

"We announce that you're my ol' lady." Pausing in my pacing, I crossed my arms, waiting to see what she had to say about it. I didn't have long to wait.

"Your *what?*" She sat there with her mouth hanging open.

"My ol' lady—my woman," I said nonchalantly. Because it seemed the perfect solution to me.

"Are you insane? We barely know each other!" It was her turn to get up and pace. "You must be out of your damn mind."

Snagging her arm as she passed, I pulled her against me. Initially, she tried to push away, but I wasn't budging, and she finally gave up. Struggling, that was. She was pissed.

"I'm not crazy, I'm a Royal Bastard. That means something. With it comes a certain security for you when it comes to the person who wants you dead."

"Is it Ivan?" she asked, and I was instantly on edge.

"Ivan who?" I asked hesitantly. Something told me I wasn't going to like her answer to that question.

"Ivan Miloslavsky," she reluctantly replied. My heart stopped.

"What the actual fuck would he want to kill you for?" I had to fight roaring it out. Miloslavsky was a sick fuck who was thick in the Russian human trafficking rings. Rumor had it he was closely tied to Vladimir Solonik, who the Tonopah chapter had shut down.

"Because I refused to marry him," she said, and I damn near choked. The thought of her marrying anyone else sent a frisson of fury through me. The thought of it being Ivan Miloslavsky followed that fury with a cold chill.

"Does your father know what kind of shit Miloslavsky's into?" Not that her father was much better. Which had me wondering if she knew what her father did for a living.

She gave a disgusted huff. "Of course he does. Which is why I can't be anything to you, Ogun. It would slap a target so big on your back. Probably on your entire club. He probably already knows I'm with you right now." She dropped her head to rest on my chest. She could likely feel the pounding of my heart.

"What are you talking about?" I asked with deadly calm.

"My father called me after our date. He knew about me being with you." She lifted her head to look at me. The green in her hazel eyes was brilliant with the glisten of tears she held back.

"Fuck. You should've told me," I muttered.

"I'd halfway convinced myself to blow you off if you asked me out again. Then you'd be safe. I haven't talked to him in almost a year. Before that, I couldn't tell you when it was. My father has been unhappy with me for years, though. He hated that I went to school to be a vet. He wanted me to marry to his advantage, and that didn't include me working. A frivolous degree would've been okay, but what I did was 'unnecessary,' so he refused to pay for it. I thought when I refused to marry Ivan, he had written me off. Evidently not."

"Is that why you're going by Baranov instead of Kalashnik?" I asked her.

She nodded. "I legally changed my name to my mother's maiden name after I turned eighteen. When I went away to college, I didn't want the association of his last name. He's... not a nice person."

Snorting, I gave her an incredulous look. "That's being generous." Again, I wondered how much she knew.

Her jaw clenched and her nostrils flared as a single tear escaped. "Trust me. I'm fully aware. When I was fifteen years old, my virginity earned him a cool million."

If I thought I was furious before, hearing her own father had sold her virginity made me want to decimate anything around me. It took everything I had to contain my rage. Still, the pots hanging in the kitchen rattled and the salt and pepper shakers flew to the floor and rolled before I reined myself in.

Kira shoved back and spun around to stare at the kitchen. "What the hell was that?"

Fuck.

"What was what?" I asked as if I had no clue.

"Don't tell me you didn't hear that? The pots are still swaying, for fuck's sake!" Her arm swung out to motion toward the pots in question. "And the salt and pepper are on the floor!"

I'd learned the hard way not to have ones that were breakable. A scratching at the back door told me that Zaka had sensed my briefly out-of-control emotions.

"Earthquake?" I asked with a furrowed brow, praying she'd believe that crock of shit. She stepped back from me, and I immediately missed her warmth.

"Bullshit. Ogun, is your house haunted?" Her wide eyes were almost comical as she quickly jumped back into my arms as she scanned the house. I couldn't help the chuckle that slipped out. "It's not funny!"

"The house isn't haunted," I assured her with a grin. "Not exactly." I wasn't sure if she was ready to learn the depths of my abilities. Most people couldn't handle it and chalked the shit my brothers and I could do up to stuff you saw in the movies. Fictional. Which was why we kept our shit carefully guarded. She was the first person I'd let it slip around that wasn't family or club.

Well, the only one to live to tell about it anyway.

"Then what the hell was that?"

"If you go along with my plan, not only will I be able to keep you safe, I'll tell you what that was about. Deal?"

She appeared to consider my request. Then she asked, "What exactly would I have to do to be your ol' lady, and how long would we have to pretend to do it?"

I gripped her jaw firmly between my thumb and fingertips, ensuring she listened closely.

"This wouldn't be temporary. You would wear my mark. You would be mine."

She swallowed hard as I paused.

"Forever."

TEN

Kira

"I REALLY WISH I HATED YOU"—BLINK 182

"Ogun," I tried to reason with him. "You can't want to tie yourself to me simply because you think it will save me from something that may or may not happen. How do I know that the information you somehow acquired is accurate?"

"Because it was my club that was approached to do the job."

If I wasn't freaked out before, that did it. Fear seeped in around me, nearly smothering me. "Excuse me? Why in the hell would you be contacted for that?"

He heaved a heavy sigh. "That's club business."

"Club business?" I asked with a raised brow as I tried to push back out of his arms. Except he held me tight.

"Yeah. Club business. That means, for your safety, I can't discuss it with you or anyone who isn't a brother. It's nothing personal." His hand smoothed my hair and tried to comfort me.

"Hmm," I said as I shook in his arms. Though I wasn't ready to let it drop, I had a feeling I wasn't getting anything else out of him. Not that I liked it, but I let it go for the moment. Swallowing down my fear, I asked, "What exactly does it mean to get your mark?"

He bit his lip, and I watched as his pupils nearly took over his eyes as his nostrils flared slightly. If I wasn't mistaken, that hard rod pressing into me got significantly thicker.

"It means that you get tattooed."

"I've never gotten a tattoo," I admitted nervously. "I've always wanted one, but never knew what I wanted."

"Oh, believe me, I noticed. The thought of my mark being the first ink on your silky skin is enough to make me want to bend you over the counter." His voice was husky with need, and I seemed to feed on his building desire.

"I might not object to that," I said in a breathy voice I barely recognized. The pulsing of my core increased as I visualized him following through with it. Anything to get me out of this nightmare I seemed to have stepped into with both feet.

He actually growled as he lifted me up and over his shoulder. I let out a surprised squeal.

"Ogun!" He ignored me. "Voodoo!" He smacked my ass, and I froze.

Before I knew it, he was setting me on the counter and his fingers were in the waistband of my pants. "Lift," he ordered. Like a lost soul, I raised my ass as he tugged my pants and underwear down in one motion. The cool granite under me had me sucking in a startled breath.

Gripping the outside of my legs, he spread them and pressed a kiss to the sensitive skin of my inner thighs. With a sigh, I fell back to rest on my hands. He dropped to his knees, and his hot breath tickled across my wet slit.

In the back of my mind, I knew we still needed to talk about what he'd just told me, but with his hands and mouth strumming me like a guitar, I couldn't collect my thoughts. When his lips latched on to my clit at the same time as he slipped two fingers into my dripping wet sheath, I fell further into the abyss.

"Oh God," I gasped. He was relentless. It was both heaven and sweet torture. The sensation overload drove me to squeeze my legs together. Of course, he was having none of it and pushed them open with his shoulders. One hand continued to work its magic, stroking the spot that had me squirming and panting as the other splayed over my lower abdomen.

The feeling of building pressure caused my breath to hitch. Higher and higher it blossomed and expanded until I exploded in a blast of pulsing energy. My chin dropped to my chest as my body folded into itself and rode the waves of bliss. On and on, he drew it out until I was left reeling in the lingering aftershocks of the most powerful climax I'd ever experienced.

He stood, wiping the glistening evidence of my orgasm off his face with the back of his hand. His eyes were heated, and I could've sworn I actually saw a flicker of a flame within their icy depths.

"Absolutely stunning view," he murmured with a wicked twist of his lips.

Leaving my pants on his kitchen floor, he lifted me off the counter, carried me down a hall, and placed me reverently on the bed. Languidly, I watched him undress. With each inch of his beautiful body he exposed, my heart surged until it was nearly bursting.

Tattoos were scattered along his tanned skin, and I wanted to trace each and every one of them. He had said I was stunning, but he was a masterpiece.

Like a beast of prey, he moved onto the bed and up my body.

My breath froze. Muscles rippling, he stalked me. Only when he hovered over me could I inhale.

Nudging into my slick opening, he made two shallow strokes before plunging deep. We both gasped as he pushed in the final inch, and I could feel his shaft stretching me in the most perfect way.

"Fuck. If I could stay here for the rest of my life, I'd die a happy man," he groaned into my mouth as he pressed his lips to mine. With each thrust, his body owned mine. The world outside our little bubble ceased to exist. The only thing I was cognizant of was the glide of sweat-slick skin against skin. Sensation was my closest friend.

Our love song was soft gasps and needy groans.

"Yes," I whispered as I clung to him.

There was nothing rushed, allowing for crystalline focus on every movement. My tongue devoured the salty taste of his skin. My senses were filled with the unique, carnal scent of our coupling. There was no him, nor me. There was only us. One body, one heart, one mind.

How he maintained that slow, steady assault on my being, I couldn't fathom. But I sure as hell drank it in and allowed myself to drown in the ecstasy that he summoned.

I'd never been so amazed and complete in all my life.

And as he gave his final forceful strokes within me, my back arched and I became whole.

Crazy as it may sound, it was like realizing I'd been stumbling around in life with half a heart. Barely living. In his arms, with his trembling body cocooning mine and his beautiful lips dotting soft kisses on my skin—I was alive.

But for how long?

ELEVEN

Voodoo

"LONELY IS THE NIGHT"—BILLY SQUIER

After feeling as if I'd emptied my soul within her, I damn near collapsed on top of her. Not wanting to cause her pain, but barely able to function, I rolled over. She whimpered when I slipped free of her heat, and I pulled her against me, where she curled into my side and laid her head over my pounding heart.

"What the hell was that?" she asked as her fingers traced the tattoos on my chest. She still sounded slightly winded.

"That was you being mine," I replied before kissing her on the head. She was perfectly molded to my side, and I reveled in it.

She gave a snorting laugh, and I held her tighter for a moment.

"So what kind of tattoo do I have to get? Can it be cool at least? And where does it have to be?" Her questions hit one after the other, and I debated if I should tell her exactly what she had to get or if I should just get it done and ask for forgiveness.

Flipping her long blonde hair to the side, I trailed my fingers over the sensitive nape of her neck to the base where it connected to her soft shoulders. "Here."

"On my neck? But people will see it!" She raised her head to look at me in wide-eyed disbelief. The curtain of silky hair fell to tickle across my shoulder and arm.

"That's the whole point, babe. People will see it and know that you're protected by the Royal Bastards. They'll know you're mine." My fingers sifted through her hair as I avoided a deeper discussion on the matter.

"Do I get a say so in what it is?"

I sighed. "Sort of."

"Meaning?"

"My road name is Voodoo. I was thinking a Mardi Gras mask." There was more, but I wasn't sure she'd go for it if I told her.

"That sounds like it would be pretty," she said with a shy smile.

"It will be. I promise."

She was silent for a minute.

"Okay. So when do we do this?" My eyes shot to hers. I'd be lying if I said I wasn't surprised that she was so readily agreeing.

"So that's a yes? You're in? There's no backing out." I clutched the hair at the back of her head, holding her to look me in the eye. I needed to ensure she was paying attention to me. She needed to understand that if she became my ol' lady, there was nothing I wouldn't do for her and no going back. Whatever shit came our way, I would do my very best to protect her from it. Whatever ups and downs we had, we took them together.

She rested her chin on her hand over my heart. "It might make me seem a little off my rocker, but when I'm with you it feels… right. Like this is meant to be. Even though I barely know you."

She had no idea.

"Besides, even if this goes to shit, it's still a cool tattoo that I could handle having without you," she reasoned. There wouldn't be a without me, but I kept quiet.

"Do you feel safe with me?"

"Yes." Her answer was firm. No hesitation.

"How long have you known me?"

"Almost a year. Well, about nine months. Since you got Zaka."

"Shit. Be right back." She'd reminded me that I'd left the dogs outside while we'd talked. Well, we had talked first and then I'd poured my emotions out to her in the only way I knew how. I wasn't always great with words.

Unashamedly naked, I climbed out of bed, made my way through the house, and opened the inner doggie door. The pups darted in the minute I opened it. Zaka had probably been lying outside the door since he sensed my minor breakdown.

"Hey, kids. Should we go see if Mom is hungry?" I asked the two dogs as they sat obediently listening to me. Rewarding them, I gave them each a treat. Calling her "Mom" to the fucking dogs had slipped out, but I was again hit with the desire to see her pregnant with my kid.

"Fuck," I muttered. I'd never been so twisted up by a chick. Then again, my visions had shown me that she was the one. The problem was, if I didn't figure out a way to ensure her safety, I was going to lose her.

The entire way back to the room, the dogs shadowed me, nails clicking on the tiles. Once we hit the room, they took off. There was no time to call them back, because right when they launched, I saw she was sleeping.

"No!" I whisper-yelled, but they were already licking her.

Thankfully, she was giggling at the attention. "Sorry, I didn't realize you were sleeping until they were already midair."

"It's okay," she said to me. Then she was done with the overexuberant attention. "Enough, Sasha."

"Zaka! Settle!" Though he was relatively young, Zaka was extremely smart and listened well. He quickly dropped to the bed, panting happily. Sasha turned, went to the end of the bed, and curled up next to him.

"Aww, look! They're friends." She grinned and sat up. My mouth suddenly dry, I stared at her bare tits and blinked like a fucking idiot.

It was almost comical when she realized she was sitting there naked as hell. She flushed bright pink and jerked a pillow over to cover herself. I wanted to pout. Okay, maybe I did a little.

Clearing my throat, I said, "You don't have to cover up on my account. I was enjoying the view. And I have a feeling those two are gonna be more than friends one day." A wry grin curled my lips.

She bit her lower lip, and her brow furrowed in hesitation. "Maybe?"

I couldn't help it. She was so goddamn cute, I laughed as I climbed into the bed. Gently, I pushed her to lie down and settled over her on my elbows. "Mmm-hmm. Okay."

Desperately needy, I pressed my hips into her, reveling in the jolt that hit when I slid through her wet core. I didn't dive inside, despite how badly I wanted to go again. Instead, I simply rested there, enjoying the feel of her heat on my shaft.

Twirling a strand of her hair, I considered my next words. "I know this must seem extremely sudden. But there's been something about you that drew me from day one. It's no secret I've been trying to get you to go out with me since then. You have to know, this isn't only about keeping you safe."

Trying to gauge her response, I glanced up at her beautiful face. Uncertainty warred with a softness in her brilliant hazel eyes. She took my breath away, and I wasn't used to that. I was a hard man in a bold and ruthless club. My past sculpted me into a man that didn't deserve her, but because of who I was, I was going to take her anyway.

"I'm scared," she whispered. "I feel like I'm damned if I do and damned if I don't."

"What are you talking about?"

"If I tell you I can't do this, I stand the very real possibility of dying. I'm guessing because of who my father is—yet, if they only knew, he could honestly not give less of a shit about me unless it benefits him. Then again, if I say yes to you, I risk my father losing his shit and going after you and your club." She reached her hand up and trailed her fingertips along my jaw, then down my neck to my chest. Her palm rested above my heart.

I dropped my head long enough to kiss the silky skin above her heart, then held her gaze. "Regardless of your choice, I'll do my best to keep you safe. Even if it means I die doing it."

She sucked in a sharp breath. "Ogun," she whispered, but before she could utter another word, I silenced her with a kiss. When I was sure she'd be quiet, I raised my head.

"No. I can't tell you how I know that you're meant to be mine, because you wouldn't believe me if I tried. What I can tell you is, this is real for me. I mean, my feelings... and all." It was so hard to say the words. Especially when they made me sound like some kind of pussy from one of those smut books my mother read. "Yet, I don't want you to make your decision based on fear. I meant what I said—if you become my ol' lady, it's not temporary."

"Okay?" It came out as a question, so I knew she wasn't agreeing with what I wanted. Not yet, anyway.

"Hey, think about it for a bit. Meanwhile, are you hungry? It's getting late, and I haven't eaten. Wasn't sure if you had." Unable to resist her allure, I nipped and teased her neck with my tongue. Each gentle bite had her arching further into me and sexy sighs slipping from her, interspersed with needy moans.

"Is that a yes?" I murmured against the smooth skin of her neck.

"Umm, what was the question?" she asked drunkenly.

I grinned triumphantly against her, yet I pulled back and waited for her to open her eyes. "Come on. Let me feed you. You're going to need your strength tonight."

"That sounds fabulous," she said with a sigh.

Grabbing a clean T-shirt from my drawer, I slipped it over her head. "You want me to cook something or are you good with sandwiches?"

"Sandwiches are perfectly fine with me." The satiated smile on her face brought out my smile. Foregoing underwear, I pulled on my jeans and padded to the kitchen. The dogs remained on the bed, snoring happily.

We were quiet while I prepared the food and while we ate. When she finished, she stood and came over to grab my plate. Before she could take it, I took her hand in mine and tugged her into my lap.

Hooking my hand behind her neck, I pulled her in for a kiss. Reluctantly breaking away, I scattered kisses along her cheeks. The last one, I pressed to the pulse I could see on her throat.

"I want you inked as soon as possible. Both for my own selfish reasons and for your safety," I said against her skin.

"Wow. Um, okay? Do we need to make an appointment?" she asked, and I chuckled.

"No. I have a guy. He'll get you in immediately."

"Like now?" she squeaked and jumped a little, causing her thigh to press harder against my dick.

Stifling a groan, I tapped on my phone screen to see the time. Then I looked at her. "Yeah. Like now."

"Fuck. Ogun. This is so fast. It's a little scary."

"Maybe. But I'm not one to beat around the bush. I tried, but the last several months drove me insane. Every time I saw you, I wanted to bend you over and fuck you until you couldn't see straight. When I realized I wasn't thinking of other women, and…." I sighed, because I wanted to tell her about my vision, but I wasn't sure if it was the time.

"Ogun, I've thought you were hot as Hades since the first time you stepped into the clinic with Zaka. But I'm a new vet, and I didn't want to jeopardize that by having inappropriate thoughts about, or relations with, a client." She gave a teasing grin, which faded as she saw the seriousness on my face. My grip on her neck tightened possessively.

"Something happened that told me you were the one, and I realized I didn't want to wait. I'm sorry you aren't getting the flowers, pretty words, dates, and you know—all that sappy shit girls like. But this is me telling you that as long as you're mine, I'll protect you with everything in me. I'll be faithful to you and only you. I'll worship your body and your mind. I'm a hard man, but I love just as hard." It was the closest I'd come to admitting the feelings that stirred in the depths of my soul for her.

"Damn, sometimes you say things that take my breath away and I realize you're so much more than a pretty face." With a smirk, she kissed the tip of my nose, and I smacked the part of her ass that reached out past my thigh.

"You're goddamn right, I'm more than a pretty face." I

dove into her neck, rubbing my stubble against her tender skin, causing her to giggle and squeal. Then I sent a text to Chains.

He replied within seconds.

Chains: I'm at the shop cleaning up but I'll wait for you if you wanna come over

Me: Be there ASAP

Chains: Roger that

"Let's go." I swatted her ass again.

Biting her lip, she raised a brow and nuzzled me with her nose. "You keep doing that, and we aren't going anywhere." The whispered words tickled against my ear and half had me canceling with Chains. Instead, I tapped her shoulder with a finger.

"Get dressed," I instructed her. "I'll take care of the dishes. Wear something comfy."

"Yes, sir," she snarked with a sexy curl of her lips.

"Woman. Don't test my limits. You're going to have me breaking all kinds of speed limits on the way there if you don't stop that shit."

"Why would you have to speed because of that?" she asked with a laugh.

"Because I'll lay you on this table and shove my fat dick in that pussy until your eyes roll. That will take a few minutes we don't have right now." My hand squeezed the luscious globe of her ass I'd been abusing. The purr that rolled off her tongue told me she'd let me too.

"You sure we have to go tonight?" Hunger filled her eyes as she leaned back to look at me.

"Get dressed."

"Okay." With one last smirk, she got up and headed to my room. Blazing heat surging through me, I watched the way my shirt showed the movement of her ass as she walked away.

Fucking hell, she was going to kill me with that body—but what a way to go.

Making quick work of the dishes, I returned to the bedroom to find her in the bathroom, brushing her teeth. She had on those sexy legging things and a shirt that fell off one shoulder.

With images in my head of the ink she'd soon have, I dressed, shoved my gun in the holster, and grabbed my wallet and keys.

"You ready?" I asked as she came out of the master bath.

She inhaled deeply, then blew it out in a huff. "I guess so."

When she wrinkled her nose as she slipped on a pair of Vans, I couldn't help myself. Framing her face, I made her look at me. "You realize this is just a technicality, right? You're already mine, but I want there to be no question."

The pink of her tongue snuck out as she wet her lips and nodded. I swooped in for one last kiss.

"Zaka. Guard." His ears perked up, but his head remained on his paws. Sasha was laid out on her side with her back against his. They'd obviously worn each other out while Kira and I had been busy earlier.

I locked up the house, and we got on my bike. I handed my helmet back to her, making a mental note to get her one of her own. Though I hated them, she wouldn't be on the back of my bike without one if I could help it.

As we drove into the night, I teemed with restless energy.

Something was coming, and I didn't think I was going to like it.

I'd read the cards when we got back to see if I was able to get any answers. Maybe throw the bones.

Until then, I pushed the feeling aside.

Kira was about to be branded with my mark.

A huge grin spread across my face.

TWELVE

Kira

"CHANGE (IN THE HOUSE OF FLIES)"—DEFTONES

"Holy fucking shit!" I said as the tattoo gun seemed to be scraping off my skin. Initially, I thought it wasn't bad. It wasn't long before the back of my neck was burning and I was gritting my teeth. "Did it feel like this with all of your tattoos?" I gasped as my eyes found Ogun through the hole of the massage chair I sat on.

Chains chuckled from behind me, and Ogun gave a wry smile. "Pretty much."

"Jesus! What the hell is wrong with you?" I asked with bugging eyes. My hands clutched the edge of the armrests, and I bit down on my lip.

Both men laughed again. When I'd found out who Ogun's tattoo artist was, I'd almost refused. Because I was embarrassed as hell. I was so thankful that neither of them had mentioned the first night I'd met Chains.

"We're almost done, babe," Chains said in his slightly

gravelly voice. His large inked hands were surprisingly gentle, except for the torture device he was wielding against my poor skin. I'd found myself wondering if the man had ink everywhere but his dick. Because after the show I'd caught at the party, I knew there was nothing on it. My face flamed at the memory.

"It doesn't look stupid, does it? You're not putting something people are going to laugh at, are you?" I asked for about the twentieth time since we'd started. In all honesty, I was shocked that I'd agreed to get a tattoo essentially sight unseen. My first one, at that.

"I promise," he murmured. I could tell by the way Ogun looked at him that they were staring at each other in a silent conversation. An uneasy feeling blossomed in my chest.

"Ogun?" My voice had risen an octave by the end of his name. He was leaning against the wall as he watched over Chains as he worked. I glared at him petulantly.

"You'll see it when he's done. It's turning out pretty sick. Chains does good work, don't worry."

Chains again chuckled. A huffing growl escaped me as he wiped my skin for the seven thousandth time.

After an undeterminable time passed, he wiped the area at the base of my neck for possibly the fifty thousandth time. "You wanna see it before I cover it up?"

"Yes!" exploded from my bruised lips.

I hopped up off the chair, and he handed me a mirror. I used it and the one on the wall to look at the first tattoo I'd ever received. Once I realized what it said, I shouted, "Voodoo! What the fuck?"

"Chill, babe. It's beautiful," he said with an unrepentant smile. My jaw was on the floor as I looked into the mirror again.

Yeah, it really was beautiful, but holy fucking shit! There

was a delicate Mardi Gras mask brilliantly colored in red and black. Above it were the words "Property of" while below it was "Voodoo." It was truly a work of art, but the words nearly had me hyperventilating.

"Cover it," I said in a muted voice as I dropped the mirror to the counter.

"What do you think?" asked Chains, and I whirled on him with narrowed eyes, because I was sure I heard laughter in his question. He obviously thought this was funny, but his expression was nothing but expectant as he waited for my answer.

"You do good work. It's beautiful," I said tightly, because it was the truth. It really was. Then my eyes flashed to Voodoo. He had a smug look on his handsome face, but his ass was mine as soon as we got home.

Home.

Holy shit, I hadn't been at his house one night and I was thinking of it as home. Then it dawned on me; we hadn't discussed what our living arrangements would be, or what me being "his" entailed as far as accommodations.

Chains carefully dressed the new tattoo.

My nostrils flared, and my teeth were grinding as I watched my "keeper" hand Chains a wad of bills.

"Brother, you don't owe me anything," Chains said as he tried to hand the money back.

"Bullshit. This is your job, and if you won't take it as payment, then it's a tip for a job exceptionally well done."

Chains rolled his eyes, but obviously realized he'd be fighting a losing battle if he didn't take it. "Thanks, brother. You gonna come in so we can start on that sleeve?"

Voodoo grinned. "Soon," he said. In my mind, I was referring to him as Voodoo because I was pissed as fuck at him.

Chains gave me an after-care instructions sheet and explained everything to me. He gave me a small tin of whatever it was he'd said to put on it. Honestly, everything he said was a dull murmur over the incessant buzzing I still heard in my head. Maybe that was my fuming anger.

Without saying a word, I headed out to wait for Voodoo by the door. My arms were crossed angrily in front of me, and I tapped one foot impatiently.

I had to braid my hair to the side so it wouldn't be across the covered but tender area of my neck. I pulled the helmet on in a huff and got on behind him. He had the nerve to chuckle as he started the bike. The vibrations of his laughter gave him away as I pressed my chest to his back and wrapped my arms around his leather vest.

The whole way back to his house, I so wanted to fuck with him by grabbing his junk, but I was afraid he'd wreck. I'd find another way to get even.

We'd parked in the garage and the door was slowly rolling down before he spoke. "Babe, I know you're upset," he began.

I jumped off the bike. "Upset? You think I'm upset? I'm fucking livid, Ogun Dupré!"

Laughing, he took the helmet I shoved into his stomach and hung it from the bike. I stormed to the door, only to realize I didn't know the code to get in. It took the wind out of my sails, and I deflated.

He reached around me and punched the code in slow enough for me to see what it was. "You want me to know your code?"

"Of course. It's your home now too. Unless you want to find a different place. My duplex was fine for me and Zaka, but maybe we need a bigger place for the kids." He opened the door, and Sasha barreled into me like I'd been gone for forty days and nights.

"Kids?" I asked in shock.

He commanded the dogs to sit, then motioned to Zaka and Sasha. "Yeah. The kids."

At their expectant expressions, I caved, and my anger began to dissipate.

"Oh my God, this is for real, huh?" I inhaled sharply and released it in a shuddering exhale. His hands gripped my shoulders, and he gently turned me to face him. One hand lifted my chin to look up at him.

"Did you really doubt that it was? When I say something, I mean it. Yeah, this is for real."

"So I went from my father owning me and using me to being owned by you," I said as my eyes filled with tears. The devastation I felt was choking me.

Disbelief flickered across his face. "Fucking hell, Kira. That's not what that means. I don't own you, but you are mine. That tells every motherfucker out there that if a hair on your head gets harmed, they answer to me. And there will be nowhere they can hide from my wrath."

Still unsure, I quietly turned and went to the bedroom. I dug out a pair of pajamas and got ready for bed. Not waiting on Ogun, I climbed into bed and curled on my side. My emotions were a jumbled mess.

Right as I was dozing off, the bed dipped behind me, and his stupidly sculpted arm reached around to tug me into the curve of his body. "You're on my side of the bed," he murmured in my ear before he kissed the top of my shoulder to the side of the bandage.

Too tired to care, I absorbed his warmth and slipped into a restless sleep.

The next day, I was still upset with him. After I took care of the dogs, I wanted to just head to work. Unfortunately, my vehicle was at home. It was the same reason I hadn't grabbed my bag and Sasha and headed home the night before.

After dressing in my red scrubs that were standard for the clinic, I waited for him to finish the call he was on. Because I didn't want to answer a bunch of questions, I wore the back of my hair down, with only the top put up to keep it out of my face.

Once he ended his call, he gave me a wary glance. "You still mad?"

I grunted noncommittally. Wisely, he held his tongue as he pulled his boots on and slipped his arms into his vest, that I'd learned was called a cut. The night before, Chains had explained it was short for "cut-off" from when they had cut the sleeves off a jacket.

"Sasha, come," I commanded. She obeyed, but she gave me a pouty sad-eyed gaze before looking back to Zaka.

"Zaka, guard," he said. The black dog dropped to his haunches but also seemed to be pouting.

Before we got in the Jeep, he took the cut off again, and I was confused. Why put it on, only to take it off again before he got in the vehicle? He folded it inside out and settled it between him and the seat belt. Like he actually buckled the thing into the seat belt by his hip.

Sasha was subdued the entire way to the clinic—as if she not only missed Zaka but was feeding off the tension between me and Ogun.

"I'll pick you up at closing?" he asked me.

"Geneva can come get me," I tried.

"Let me rephrase that. I'll see you when the clinic closes," he said firmly. My gaze found his, and I froze as his hand wrapped around the back of my neck and pulled me close. "I'm giving you today to wrap your head around all this. I said you were mine, and I meant it. I also wasn't playing around when I said it wasn't temporary. I finally got you where I want you, and I'm not letting go. Got it?"

Eyes wide, heart hammering, and lungs seized, I nodded.

"Good." His firm lips stole my resolve the second they assaulted mine in a sinfully wicked battle. His teeth grabbed my lip as he broke the kiss, and I sagged into him, hand clutching his plain black T-shirt. His tongue stroked across my lip that was still held in his teeth, sending a shiver of desire through me.

When he let me go, my chest was slowly heaving. It took a minute to gather my scattered brain cells. Running my tongue across my lips, I tasted him and sighed.

"How do you do that?" I rasped.

"It's a talent," he murmured with a smirk.

I was in trouble.

"I'll see you later," I said before unhooking Sasha. After I got out of the vehicle, I said, "Come."

She hopped out and waited for me to head inside. Once I had my work tote, I looked back at him. "You don't fight fair."

His sexy smile was megawatt. "Never said I did."

He waited for me to get inside before he backed out to go do whatever it was he did for the farm he worked at. I'd never really asked, but I remembered his forms had listed one of the most prominent hog farms in the area as his employer.

It was an unusually busy day that I was extremely thankful for, because it kept my mind occupied.

I should've known my father wouldn't let my "indiscretions" slide.

THIRTEEN

Voodoo

"CAGE THE BEAST"—ADELITA'S WAY

"I heard Kira is wearing your brand," Angel said with a repressed grin the second I walked into the clubhouse. He and Croc smirked from where they were playing pool, and I wanted to knock their heads together.

"Fuck, you all gossip worse than a bunch of chicks," I said with an exasperated huff as I gave Chains a disgusted eye-roll. He'd obviously been running his mouth.

"Never thought I'd see the day when Voodoo was pussy-whipped," said Ghost from the bar. Narrowing my eyes, I looked at the glass of ice water in front of him. With a smirk, I flipped him off, and the glass tipped over, spilling water all over his leg.

"You fucker!" He jumped up, standing the cup up. "That was fucking cold!"

"Quit whining. It's only water. You'll dry," I said with a smug expression. Croc chuckled, and the water on the bar gathered up and landed in the glass. Water was his thing. He could manipulate it and control it like it was a part of him.

Ghost rolled his eyes and muttered, "Show off."

"Voodoo! My office. Now," Venom said from the entry to the back hall.

"Oooo, you're in trouble!" Ghost chided with a grin. Again, I offered him a one-finger salute as the rest of my brothers laughed.

"Don't you fuckers have shit to do? I know there are jobs waiting to be completed in the shop. If you need a list of things to keep you busy, I think the shitters could use an extra deep clean." Venom loudly announced to the room. They all scattered, and I followed Venom down the hall.

He moved to stand behind his heavy wood desk. When I sat across from him, he dropped a folder in front of me with a loud smack as it hit the table.

"What's this?" I asked.

"Is it true? Kira Baranov aka Kalashnik is officially your ol' lady?"

"Yeah," I replied warily, with my fingers preparing to open the folder.

"She got your brand already?" Venom asked.

"You know she does if you're asking me if she's my ol' lady. What's in the folder?" Suddenly, I didn't feel like I wanted to see it.

"De Luca took you up on your offer. When you see what's in there, you may wish you'd sacrificed her. This could bring a whole shitload of trouble with it if you aren't careful, brother." Venom said with a serious glint in his eye.

Trepidation filled me as I flipped open the cover. Inside, were pictures that turned my stomach. With each one I flipped over, rage and hatred burned. When I'd seen the last one, he tossed three more images on the pile. They fanned slightly and I picked them up.

"De Luca said the girl lives if you can take out Grishka Kalashnik, but first, he wants Ivan Miloslavsky ruined and Anatoly Kalashnik's head in a box." My eyes lifted from the images of the three men.

"In a box, literally?" I asked with a raised brow.

"Yes. Literally."

"Done." I sifted through the repulsive images of the things her father had done until I found the one that made my blood boil.

"Who's the fat fuck?" I asked with barely repressed fury. The pens in the cup on Venom's desk rattled and fell over. Venom sighed and shook his head as he righted them.

"That's Lester Damen. He's the oldest son of former senator Frank Damen. Rich as Croesus. Twisted as fuck—whole family is." Venom spat out his reply as if it left a bad taste in his mouth.

"Tell De Luca I'll throw him in for free." I tossed the images to the desk as my lip curled.

"Voodoo...." He said my name in warning.

"No. This is not negotiable. That fucker paid a million dollars to her piece of shit father for her motherfucking virginity. She was fifteen fucking years old. I'll deliver him to hell myself if I have to, with his dick shoved so far down his throat he'll be shitting it out as he swallows." Violence radiated through me, and the need to unleash the darkness within was nearly uncontrollable. "You want to put it to a vote, that's fine. But if I have to, I'll step away from the club and do it on my own."

The beast was lunging and gnashing its teeth.

Venom set his hand on my forearm, and the room stilled. The snarling creature slunk back to its corner, and I sat breathing heavily as I stared into Venom's odd-colored eyes.

"We'll put it to the vote, but I want you to keep your shit together. You can't throw your entire life away because you are trying to protect her."

Unwavering, I met his gaze. "Yes, I absolutely can. She's mine. I had a vision about her," I admitted in a low voice. He sucked in a sharp breath.

"Voodoo, your visions aren't always exact," he tried to argue, but I was having none of it.

"My visions have become increasingly accurate over the years, and you know it. Hell, I just had the one about Axel and his ol' lady out in Arizona. You know I was spot-on with that shit." I paused. "Look, I actually saw us getting married, but I also saw her hurt. That part I need to prevent if I'm able." I ran a hand through my hair, frustrated.

"So you're basing your future and love on a vision?" Venom asked in disbelief.

"No," I said slowly, like I was talking to a three-year-old. "I already had a pretty deep attraction to her. My vision simply showed me I was on the right track with her. And that picture of Lester Damen? Burn it. That's the reason he's mine. The girl in the image is my woman, and I don't want my brothers seeing her like that."

His head dropped for a second, and I heard him mutter *"Fuck"* before he met my gaze again.

"Fine. Call church for tonight. If the brothers are on board, then Damen is yours. If they aren't? You don't touch him." His words were final, and I was left grinding my teeth. Despite my feelings, I knew he was right. My personal feelings couldn't be allowed to destroy my club. I prayed they'd be on board.

After I showed the brothers the shit that Lester Damen had been guilty of and told them what he'd done to Kira, they were well on board with my needs. Not a single one hesitated to give me their vote. The fact that Kalashnik had allowed photographs of his own daughter being raped as her oldest brother held her down was beyond repulsive.

I'd happily put a bullet between both of their eyes. That was after I had a little revenge against them and Damen.

When I pulled up outside the vet clinic, I'd intended to wait in the Jeep, but I decided there was no time like the present to show my hand. Especially if my instincts were correct and she hadn't said a word yet.

The bell on the door rang as I stepped through, and Veronica gave me a big flirtatious grin. "Hey, Voodoo. Everything okay with Zaka?" She bit her lip.

"Oh, yeah. He's great. I'm here to pick up Kira." The stunned disappointment on her young face was almost comical. It had me feeling half bad for her. I'd never led her on, though, so I didn't feel guilty.

I heard nails rapidly clicking on the floor before Sasha came from the back hall. She excitedly dove for me, and I chuckled but made her obey. "No, Sasha. Settle."

She immediately sat, and I could've sworn she was grinning at me as her tongue lolled out of her mouth. I rewarded her with affection as I scratched and ruffled her fur.

"You have all the women eating out of your hand," said Veronica as she leaned over the counter. I heard a snort and turned to the hall where Kira stood with her arms crossed. Her sassy attitude made me smirk.

"All but one, it would seem," I said, trying not to laugh as she rolled her eyes. "You about ready, babe?" I threw that last bit in to alleviate any question of where my feelings were aligned. Veronica sighed.

"I thought you'd wait outside," Kira huffed. I looked up at her from where I crouched, scratching her dog's belly.

"You thought wrong." I shrugged, and laughter slipped out when she rolled her eyes and turned to Veronica to ensure there wasn't any emergencies that had popped up.

She gathered her bag and Sasha's leash and snubbed me as she went to the door. As she stepped out, she waved. "See you tomorrow, Veronica."

"Not sure what you did to piss her off, but her favorite dessert is turtle cheesecake." Veronica gave me a good-natured wink, and I nodded.

"Appreciate that," I replied with a wave and followed Kira out. She was already in the Jeep with Sasha buckled in the harness in the back seat.

"You remember what I said?"

"About what?"

"I told you I was giving you some time to get your head straight. You agreed to be my ol' lady, with all it entailed."

"You didn't say I would be looked at as property! That's degrading!" She fumed.

"And I told you, it's not like that. That brand you got on your neck protects you. There's not a motherfucker alive that will risk my wrath to fuck with you. I don't own you. You're not a fucking dog. But make no mistake about it, Kira—you are mine."

Not giving her time to argue further, I backed out and drove toward her house to get her vehicle. When we stopped at her place, I went in with her. Geneva was watching TV.

"Hey, you two!" she said with a happy twinkle in her eyes.

"Hey, Geneva. Kira's moving in with me. I'll pay the next

two months of her portion of the rent so you're not left hanging," I said as Kira gasped behind me.

"Ogun! You can't do that. I'm not making you pay my bills!" I hid my smile that she didn't argue about moving in with me. Geneva made no effort to hide her huge-ass grin.

"Sounds good. I appreciate that. But if I get someone else in right away, there's no need." I waved her off. It was the least I could do for her trouble.

"Don't bother arguing," Kira said from behind me. "He does what he wants anyway."

Geneva watched the volley between Kira and me with a giggle.

"I'm glad she's figuring this out," I said with a tilt of my lips. Geneva burst out laughing. Out of the corner of my eye, I saw Kira throw her hands in the air and stomp to her room. The entire time, Sasha lay sleeping on the floor by Geneva's feet.

She acted miffed, but Kira packed all her shit in several bags and suitcases. Holding my tongue, I helped her load everything into her vehicle and the back seat of mine. On the way back to my place, I stopped into Hy-Vee and grabbed a turtle cheesecake while she waited in her vehicle. She was trying to see what I'd gotten, but I kept it well hidden.

Once we arrived at the house, Sasha and Zaka hauled ass out to the backyard.

I put all of Kira's bags in my room. Looking in my closet, I anticipated I'd need to move some of my shit to the spare bedroom closet. It would be worth it.

Kira was in the kitchen stomping around and slapping ingredients on the counter. As she went to walk past me, I grabbed her arm, bringing her to a halt.

"Look at me."

She was petulant, but she listened. Her eyes held a fire that I'd have liked to see in a different circumstance. Like one where we were both naked.

"By the time we go to bed, I want you to have this shit out of your system. I'm not gonna walk on eggshells, nor am I gonna kiss your ass. But I sure as hell will fuck it out of you. Mark my words—by tomorrow, you'll be too tired to be so sassy." Her eyes widened with every word, and the tip of her tongue traced her bottom lip. Hungrily, I watched it glide.

Palming the front of her throat, I pulled her in. I loved to feel the jump in her pulse under my fingers when I did that. It sent a powerful surge through me. My lips hit hers, and like always, we combusted.

Before I knew it, she was sitting on the edge of the counter and I was pressed hard between her legs. My hands were up her shirt, and hers were in my hair.

Finally, we came up for air. "I need to start supper if we're gonna eat," she breathlessly said.

"Maybe I'm not hungry anymore. At least not for dinner." A wicked grin curled my lips. An airy laugh slipped out of her, and she gently pushed me back.

"Well, maybe what I have planned for you requires you to fuel up," she said, then bit her lip and ducked her head. Her hands were busied with her preparations, but I spun her around and stole one more kiss from her parted lips.

"Maybe you underestimate me," I said before I nipped her neck, eliciting a squeal from her as she pulled her shoulders up.

We had dinner, but it was late.

We had dessert first.

FOURTEEN

Kira

"LIFELINES"—I PREVAIL

The past week had been surreal, yet amazing. Ogun and I had developed a routine, and each night he held me in his protective arms. I'd begun to feel invincible with him at my back. Only one night did something strange happen. He'd been midthrust as he hovered over me, and he'd literally frozen up and stared blankly.

After that he was shaken, and I worried he'd had some kind of seizure, but he didn't want to talk about it. Since then, everything had been damn near perfect.

I should've realized it was the calm before the storm and that all good things must come to an end.

Clichéd but so very true.

It had been an awful day at work. Two dogs that got bit by a timber rattlesnake came in late in the afternoon. I'd had to call Ogun and let him know I was going to be late. It was touch and go with one; the other suffered a "dry bite" and would be sore and swollen but likely just fine.

Pulling my hair out of the tight ponytail, I massaged my scalp. The headache that had been raging began to diminish. I shot off a quick text to Ogun to let him know I was almost done, then dropped my phone in the cargo pocket on my leg.

"Do you need me to help with anything?" I asked Veronica and Lexi. They were busy cleaning up after the procedure, and I hated leaving them behind to do all the grunt work. Doc was in the back with Mrs. Moran doing his final paperwork. I'd tried to offer to do it, but he didn't like letting the rest of us do his charting even though the poor guy sucked with the computer.

"No, we're good. You go home to that sexy biker of yours," Veronica said with a sly smile. Lexi was a part-time high school tech, and she turned her head to hide her giggle. They'd been teasing me all week about Ogun.

Especially after they saw the tattoo.

Dr. Moran had seemed extremely concerned at first, but when he saw how attentive Ogun had been, he'd lightened up. Ogun had been by almost every day during his break, bringing me lunch or coffee when I hit that midday slump.

I laughed. "If you're sure. Thank you for all your help today. You both did great."

"Thanks, Doc," they said in unison.

"Sasha, come," I called, and she came running from the back office. "Goodnight, Doc and Mrs. Moran!" I called down the hall. I'd already said my goodbyes when they headed to the office, but I always let him know when I was going out the door.

"Goodnight, honey!" Mrs. Moran replied as she peeked her head out the door.

One last wave, and I made my way outside. Hitting the unlock button, I walked around to Sasha's side. Though I was tired, I couldn't wait to get home to Ogun. I'd missed him something fierce that day. Especially since he'd called to say he was working through his lunch.

Right as I opened the door, a meaty hand slammed over my mouth. Immediately, I tried to scream, but his hand was so big it not only covered my mouth, it nearly occluded my nose. There was a vicious snarl from Sasha, then the man shouted.

Fighting to see what was going on, my eyes wildly scanned around me right as I heard a gunshot, followed by a yelp. Behind the filthy hand, I screamed as he dragged me backwards and I saw Sasha lying on the ground with blood all over her. Fighting for all I was worth, I tried to get back to my dog.

"Shut up, bitch, or I'll go inside and kill every one of those assholes inside. Keep fighting me, and you won't make it two miles down the road. You ain't worth much more alive than you are dead." My heart was shattering as tears poured down my face. The man shoved me in the back of a pickup with a solid metal top on it.

"Hurry up!" Another guy rasped. "And she might not be worth more alive, but it's the only way he'll show up. Now get her in the goddamn truck!"

When he went to shut the back door, I scrambled to escape. The barrel of a gun against my forehead made me go stock still. "Don't. Do. It."

For two seconds, I thought I was looking into Ogun's eyes, then the man pushed me back until I fell on my ass and slammed the door.

Pitch-black surrounded me, and I fought the panic clawing at my insides.

They drove like lunatics, leaving me to be tossed and battered around in the bed of the truck. It must have been hours before we finally stopped, and I'd cried the whole way. Nothing I tried could get the vision of Sasha bleeding onto the ground out of my head.

When the doors opened, I was so terrified, I wanted to scream.

Thanks to the bright fluorescent lights, my eyes took a minute to focus. When they did, it was like being tossed into some kind of alternate universe.

There was a man dragging me out of the back, but I couldn't stop gaping at him. It was like looking at a blond Ogun. His face was a little more weathered, and a hideous scorpion was tattooed on it. The man who'd grabbed me came around the side of the truck just as the younger one smacked me for struggling.

"Bitch, I ain't gun tell you agin!" Blinking rapidly to clear my tears, I realized they had heavy accents that sounded kind of like the people on that alligator hunting show. Though there was a strong resemblance to Ogun in the younger one, the older one was heavily scarred. The eyes were eerily the same on all three.

They had parked in an underground parking garage. Glancing around, I saw there wasn't a soul in sight. The older one was messing on a phone, but all I heard was him muttering about no signal down where we were.

"Come on. He knows we here by now, anyway."

"Move!" the younger one told me as he shoved me toward an elevator door at the other end of the garage.

It seemed to be a service elevator and essentially nondescript. Once we stepped off into a back hall several stories up, a sense of familiarity began to creep in.

The older one grabbed me by the hair and jerked me back. A huge knife was held to my throat. "Get the door, Skid."

The one called Skid carefully opened the door, poked his

head out, then motioned for us to proceed. The dread that blossomed in my chest was smothering me.

Because I knew exactly where I was.

A ridiculously tall door swung open at the end of the hall. Standing in the doorway, arms crossed, wearing an expensive, immaculate suit, was the man who should've protected me.

Before he punched me in the face, I heard him murmur, "Welcome home, *daughter*."

I awoke lying on the floor of my old room as if I'd been tossed in. My head was pounding, and nausea swirled through me. Unsteady, I got to my feet and stumbled clumsily to the bathroom.

My knees protested the concussion of hitting the marble floors as I hurled into the commode. The heaves continued in their attempt to turn me inside out, well after there was anything left to bring up.

"Oh, God," I whimpered as I carelessly lay my head on the seat. By the time I believed it was safe to get up, my legs had gone to sleep. Barely able to move one foot in front of the other without crying, I painfully made my way to the sink.

I was a mess. Black streaks from both my mascara and whatever had been in the back of that truck covered my face, arms, and scrubs. My eyes were swollen and red. Hair, wild and ratted, stood on end. Some of the black crap from the truck was in it too.

Dizziness engulfed me, and I gripped the edge of the sink. My head swiveled to the door when it stopped, and I took a few hesitant steps into the bedroom. The door was only about fifteen feet away, but it seemed like miles.

Slowly, I made my way to it. My heart fell when the door was locked, but in all honesty, I'd expected it. Not that I hadn't been hopeful. It didn't stop me from shaking the door and pounding on the wood.

Of course, no one came.

I tried the balcony doors, but they were locked as well. Not that I would've had anywhere to go. The balcony ran all the way around the penthouse, but it was innumerable stories up. Unless I could fly, I wouldn't have been able to do anything but fall to my death.

Glancing around, I found my room was as I had left it the last time I'd been home, almost two years ago. It might be incredibly sumptuous, but it was a prison nonetheless. A gilded cage for a broken bird.

Part of me wanted to curl up in a ball and retreat inside my head as I'd become accustomed to as a young girl. Except the other part of me—the part that had a beautiful, badass tattoo on her neck—demanded I fight.

Filled with newfound resolve, I shuffled back to the bathroom, holding on to the furniture and walls to stay upright. Dizziness consumed me, and my legs were now painful as feeling returned to them. Once I got in there, I closed the door, locked it, turned on the hot water, and stripped. My pants hit the floor with a thud, and my brow furrowed in confusion.

In slow motion, I picked them up and found the source of the weight. My phone that I'd forgotten was in there.

Shit.

I could've called for help after they'd taken me. I wanted to cry all over again.

When I pressed the screen to wake it, I wanted to wail with the unfairness. It was nearly dead.

"It's okay." I started a pep-talk with myself. "Nearly dead isn't dead."

Then I saw I'd missed several calls from Ogun, but my phone hadn't rung the entire time. It made me wonder if the metal of that freaking box I'd been in had blocked my signal.

After taking a deep breath, I first dialed Ogun. Except it rang and rang before it hit voicemail. I tried again and again. I tried Geneva. Voicemail for her too. Glancing at the time and the sun barely breaking through the Chicago skyline, I realized she was likely already at work. No one I tried was answering.

"Are you serious?" I huffed on a breathless sob. I considered calling my mother, but she wouldn't be any help, because I knew she was in Fiji with my aunt.

Deciding I'd leave Ogun a message, I called again. It rang and rang. Voicemail picked up, but right as I said, "Ogun, I'm—" the phone went silent.

"No. No, no, no, no, no!" My head dropped until my chin nearly rested on my chest. A quick search of all the drawers for a charger I might've left behind left me empty-handed.

"It's okay," I assured myself again. "I'm going to shower and get my head straight."

Except when the hot water hit my skin, the tears started again. Melding with the water, they trailed down my face and to the drain. Images flashed through my mind of Sasha lifeless on the ground, then of Ogun as he'd stared into my eyes the last time he'd made love to me. Knowing I'd likely never see them again, I slid down the marble wall and sobbed.

FIFTEEN

Voodoo

"LOVE BITES"—DEF LEPPARD

Hours earlier....

As I finished up supper, I glanced at the clock. Kira should've been home. With all the dreams I'd been having about her being seriously hurt, I worried like crazy. The strange thing was, she was always wearing something different, but it was almost always white. Right when I picked up my phone, it began to ring with the number of the vet clinic.

"Did your phone die?" I asked with a grin.

"Mr. Dupré?" It was Dr. Moran. My smile dropped.

"Yes?"

"There's been a… uh, situation. The police are here. Sasha was shot and Kira is missing," he said, sounding like he might've been crying. My heart dropped as his words hit me.

"What are you talking about?" I was already pulling the food out of the oven and shutting everything off. As he explained what he knew, I grabbed my keys, shrugged on my cut, and pulled on my boots. "Zaka, guard!" I commanded as I went out to the garage.

"I'm on my way." I ended the call, shot off a text to Venom, and was down the road within seconds. The entire way there, I stewed. I told myself there was a mistake. There had to be a logical explanation.

There were flashing lights as I pulled up. Kira's vehicle sat there with the passenger-side door open. Doc was talking to one of the officers by the front of it. I jumped off my bike and started toward him.

One of the cops tried to stop me by putting a palm to my chest. Irate, I looked down at where his hand was on my cut. "Get. Your. Hand. Off. Me," I bit out.

"This is a crime scene. You can't go any closer." The fucker was pissing me off. Looking around for Officer Kellogg or one of the others that worked with us, I was disappointed to see none of them were there.

Then I heard my name called from down the side of the building. Leaning back so I could see, I saw that Veronica was hanging out of one of the employee entrances. "His dog is in here," she said with a sweet smile to the asshole cop.

Shooting him a snide grin, I jogged back to where she held the door for me. As soon as I was inside, she pulled it closed. "What the hell is going on?" I asked her. She was already moving down the hall, so I followed.

"Sasha was shot. Dr. Baranov—sorry, Kira—had just left with her, and we heard the gunshot. At first we weren't sure what it was. When we looked out the back door to see if we could see anything, we noticed Kira's passenger door was open and called for her. When we didn't see anything, we called for Sasha.

Nothing. Then we went around the vehicle and saw Sasha on the ground. We called the cops, and Doc Moran operated to try to save her."

"What about Kira?"

She looked over her shoulder with a pained expression. "We don't know."

As we walked, I pulled out my phone and tried to call her. Voicemail.

Twice more, same thing. Frustrated, I shoved my phone in my pocket.

We turned a corner and stepped into a procedure room. My heart ached at seeing Sasha's normally lively form lying so still. No matter how tough I thought I was, that proved I was a bit of a softy. Tears filled my eyes.

"She's still sedated," Veronica said behind me, and I whipped back around in shock. She gave me a sad smile. "She's going to be okay. She's going to be hurting, and it'll be a long road ahead, but she'll be okay."

"Can I have a minute?" I asked gruffly.

She nodded, then stepped out, sliding the glass door closed. I pulled out my phone.

"Hey, brother. What's up? Your text was pretty vague."

"I have a problem."

"Talk to me." Venom said, his tone immediately going serious. In the background, I heard Raptor ask who it was. "Voodoo," he told him.

"Kira was abducted from the clinic as she was leaving. Sasha, her dog, was shot and left for dead. I need Facet to see what he can find out." I was furious. Someone was going to pay for this shit.

"I'll get him on it. Call me back if you get any news."

"Roger that." I ended the call and stepped closer to Sasha, who I could now see was breathing. My fingers sifted through her thick fur. "It's gonna be okay, girl. We're gonna find your momma. I promise."

My chest ached so bad I could hardly move. Each breath was agony as I tried to hold my shit together. A rattle from the stuff on the walls told me I wasn't doing very well.

More than my next breath, I wanted to hunt down whoever had done this, but I had fuck all to go on. As I continued to run my fingers through Sasha's coat, I started to get that familiar hazy feeling.

Part of me welcomed it; part of me was afraid of what I would see.

The air sucked out of my lungs, and I fought to stay upright. It was the same as the dream I'd had as a little boy. I'd all but forgotten about it until it slammed into me. What I hadn't realized then was that the woman in my dream was Kira. She was dressed in white and calling for me. She reached out her hand as she cried on a bed.

What I'd learned since the first time it had happened was to take in the details present in my visions. Sometimes I could see more than others.

There was a floor-to-ceiling window behind her, to the side of her bed. What I saw told me where she was. At least in a general aspect.

Fuck.

Coming out of the vision, I had to shake my head to clear it. I needed to get on the road. Opening the door, I called out to Veronica. I was dialing my prez as I did.

"What's wrong?" she asked as she popped out of another room, sounding worried.

"I have to go. I might know where Kira is. Take care of Sasha?" Venom was saying my name as I spoke.

"Yes! Go!" Veronica said in a rush. Without waiting, I rushed out the door I'd come in.

"Prez, I think her father has her," I said in a near-whisper.

"Shit. Raptor, I need you to do something for me," he said. I heard Raptor reply in the background.

"I'm on my way. Be there shortly." I ended the call and got on my bike. The cop that had tried to stop me before gave me a dirty look. I wanted to flip him off, but I couldn't be bothered. I tore out of the lot and dared any of them to try to catch me.

Making it to the clubhouse in record time, I parked haphazardly and raced inside. Angel and Ghost were coming out, and I plowed into them, turning sideways to slide between them, and kept moving.

Though I heard them call out, I was focused on making it to Venom and Raptor. Right as I was headed into his office, Venom called to me from the chapel.

By the time I stepped through the door, Ghost and Angel were on my heels. They must've notified the others, because everyone that had been close came in after them.

"Voodoo, I need you to sit down. Raptor wants to try something." My gaze darted from one to the other before I warily sat. They had the chair Venom had indicated pulled out, and Raptor sat in one facing me.

My agitation was simmering hot under the surface of my skin.

"Bear with me. I don't know if this will work, but I want to try." Raptor reached out and held my hand. It shook in his, and I tried to steady it. He closed his eyes and was silent for a few minutes.

"It's not working. I think he's too angry. Or maybe it just won't work at all." Raptor turned to look at Venom, who came closer. He crouched down and stared at me.

His hand wrapped around my forearm, and I jumped. Tilting his head, he narrowed his eyes, and I eased. In the back of my mind, I knew what he was doing, but I became languid as I sat there.

After I'd calmed, I realized what they were trying to do. Normally, Raptor would simply focus on a remote or distant target and he could sense coordinates and details of the area. Except he needed to know generally what he was looking for. In this case, I was the only one who knew. It was different for him to try to do it through one of my visions, and I wasn't sure he'd have any success.

"Voodoo, I want you to think about your vision. Sift through the details you remember," Raptor said. "It was in Chicago?" he asked.

I nodded.

"Can you see what you saw in your vision?" As I relaxed further, I leaned back in the chair. I nodded.

"Okay," he said as he breathed slow and deep. After a couple of minutes, he said, "I can see Navy Pier. And the Sears Tower."

"It's Willis Tower," mumbled Facet.

"Shut the fuck up," whispered Angel. "No one cares, you smart fuck."

"I think I know the coordinates of where she is. Get me a pen and paper," Raptor murmured as he continued to hold my hand.

Venom released my forearm. I watched as Raptor used one hand to scratch out something on the paper without looking at it. Then he let go and sighed heavily. I shook off the eerie feeling.

"Facet," Venom ordered, and Facet jumped to grab the paper. He'd brought his laptop in, but I hadn't noticed it before.

It didn't take him any time at all to excitedly blurt out, "I've got it. Pricey digs. Oh, wait!" He opened a file. "I'm pretty sure this is the address I found for him. Hang on, and I'll clarify." The keys clicked at a rapid-fire pace.

"Bingo. That's where she is. We're about five and a half hours away. How many of us are going?" he asked excitedly. The kid was not only a certified genius, he was as loyal as they came. None of us had hesitated in the least to patch him in. He'd done a four-year enlistment in the military like most of us had, but he'd been into some super-secret squirrel shit. They hadn't wanted to let him get out, but he'd been done.

Hell, I guess he wasn't a kid anymore, but twenty-three was still young.

"Venom, you stay here. I'll take Angel, Facet, Ghost, Shank, and of course Voodoo. Between the six of us, I think we've got the skills we need to get her out and take care of her if we need to," Raptor offered. I knew damn well why he'd chosen the brothers he'd named. Though I prayed we wouldn't need his skills, Angel had the ability to help her if she was hurt.

"Sounds good. Voodoo? You gonna be okay to deal with this rationally?" Venom had turned to me. His eyes shifted from blue to green as he waited for me to reply. My jaw clenched as I pulled out all three of the pieces I carried on me. Ensuring the clips were fully loaded, then checking my additional two clips, I nodded.

"I'll be fine. Kalashnik isn't going to be walking out of there. I'll be talking care of his son too." My eyes raised from my immediate task. I met every brother's somber gaze. Each one gave me a nod or chin lift. They were all behind me without question.

We'd voted on it, but we'd all thought we'd have time to plan better. Fuck, I should've had Facet gathering all the necessary info to do the job the second Venom had shown me the folder. Except I'd been too wrapped up in Kira the past week.

"Kickstands up in twenty minutes, boys. Get your shit," Raptor called out. His golden eyes met mine, almost glowing. He blinked slowly. "We'll get her back."

Staring at the skull and crown on his back as he walked away, I stepped out of the chapel to call out to our prospect at the bar. "Prospect!"

"Yes, sir?" he asked as he set the rag he was wiping the bar down with to the side.

"I need you to take care of my dog." The poor guy swallowed hard when I slapped my house key on the counter but nodded.

"Yes, sir," he firmly replied. People were afraid of Zaka, and I didn't understand why. Okay, so he bit a prospect a while back. Dumb fuck shouldn't have walked in my house without knocking.

Making quick work of packing a bag from the shit in my room at the clubhouse, I was already shoving it in my saddlebag when the rest of the brothers came out.

"You ready?" Raptor asked everyone.

A round of affirmative answers ensued.

"Anyone gets any weird vibes or feelings, you share it immediately. Voodoo? You see anything, you let us know." I nodded at his instructions, as did everyone else.

"She can't be more than two, three hours tops, ahead of us," I added, based on what time Veronica said she was leaving the clinic. "But we need to get on the road."

"Voodoo, you saw her safe in her father's house, so we can only hope that doesn't change and she ends up there like you saw." Raptor laid a comforting hand on my shoulder and gave me a reassuring squeeze. Venom and everyone staying behind nodded and waited for us to take off.

"You all have the address, but Ghost will lead the way as Road Captain," Raptor instructed. "Let's go!"

Our bikes roared to life, throttles cranked as our pipes rumbled. We pulled out of the compound as a tight unit and hit the road. The miles slipped under our tires, and we stopped as little as possible.

Hang on, baby. I'm coming for you, and I'm bringing the hounds of hell with me.

SIXTEEN

Kira

"BLACK HONEY"—THRICE

"Nice to see you've cleaned up and made yourself presentable for your husband-to-be." My father's voice registered in my mind as I blinked and started to wake myself. Groggy, I raised my head in confusion.

"Ogun?" I called, though I knew he wasn't there and there would be no one to save me.

My head was jerked up by the hair, and I yelped in pain. "You thought you were too good for Ivan, yet you want to spread your legs for some biker trash? You're a fucking whore just like I always knew you'd be. Fucking *shlyukha*." Whore.

"I'm not a whore, but if I am—you made me one." My disdain for him dripped from every word.

Smack!

My head whipped to the side as he hit me. Warm wetness trickled down my chin, and I was pretty sure he'd split my lip.

"You act like you're too good for the man I chose for you, yet you fuck trash? You're a fucking slut just like your mother!" My astonishment knew no bounds that he could speak of my mother like that.

"She's been a good wife to you!" I argued with angry tears in my eyes.

"A good wife? You call a fucking whore a good wife?" He scoffed in indignation. Then he dragged me off the bed by my hair. My hands grabbed at the base of my skull in an attempt to alleviate the pain.

"She is no whore!" I screamed. My mother had been the rock I'd leaned on. She'd encouraged me to chase my dreams and not to settle for less than the best. When I was a child, she'd often tried to protect me the best she could from my father's wrath, even at the expense of her own safety. After my father had sold my virginity, she held me as I cried for weeks. She'd blamed herself for not being there. Then she'd covertly arranged counseling for me that earned her two black eyes when my father had found out months later.

"Isn't she? She fucked my own man behind my back. You call that a good wife? She thought I would never know! Then nine months later, she spits out a fucking child that looks nothing like me. She thought I wouldn't know you were Aleksandr's child!" He screamed in my ear as he hit me again. My mind whirred as shock froze me on the spot.

"What?" I whispered as my heart shattered. Not at finding out the horrid man I'd thought was my father wasn't but wondering if this Aleksandr was still alive. Did he know about me? Did he care? Had my mother loved him or was it just sex? The questions spinning in my head were endless.

"Yes, you heard correctly, which is why you've never been anything but a pawn to me. If you won't marry Ivan, then you are of no use to me. In that case, I'll at least recoup some of what you've cost me over the years."

From the floor, I looked up at him and snarled. "Oh, because the million dollars you sold my virginity for wasn't enough? What more can you do to me?"

He jerked my robe from my body so hard, I heard it rip. Trying my best to shield my nudity from him, I clutched the torn pieces in front of me. I should've kept my mouth shut.

He crouched down in front of me and trailed a finger along my cheek. I recoiled and pulled my face back, but he grabbed it in a bruising grip. In an evil whisper, he said the words that made my blood run ice-cold. "You'll go to the highest bidder, where your new owner will fuck you whenever, wherever, and however he wishes, my dear Kira."

I gasped in disgust.

"Get dressed. You have a fiancé to impress. Unless you'd like to choose option B. Oh, and if you do? Your pretty little friend you were living with will go with you. You have half an hour. If you're not dressed, I'll drag you out like you are." He gave me a cruel smile, then stood and walked away. Curling in on myself, I lay on the floor staring out the window and pleading in my mind for Ogun to find a way to save me.

No surprise that my prayers didn't get answered. Desolation unfurled in my chest, and I wanted to cry, but I wouldn't give my father—no, Grishka—the satisfaction. Numbly, I got up and splashed cold water over my face. The cut on my lip stung and started to bleed again, so I held a washcloth against it until it stopped.

Forgoing any makeup, I brushed my hair and twisted it up.

A shaky inhale did nothing to fortify my resolve.

The thought of finding a way to break the glass to the

balcony and jumping held more merit than willingly succumbing to becoming Ivan's wife. The thought of the alternative option made me want to vomit.

Dressing in the red dress my "father" had brought with him when he barged in, I curled my lip in revulsion. The low dip in the front damn near reached my belly button. The back was nothing more than a maze of strings that ended nearly at my ass crack. While I'd have happily slipped into the slinky thing for Ogun, the thought of putting it on to essentially be sold made me retch.

Diamond chandelier earrings that likely cost more than my car were my only jewelry. I wanted to shove them down Grishka's and Ivan's throats. If they choked on them, I'd dance on their graves.

"Ogun, I love you," I whispered into the still air of the room. Tears welled, and I blinked them away.

The red-bottomed shoes I slid on were like gloves on my feet, but I hated them. Each step was like one closer to my executioner. The click of the heels on the tile floors was a death knell.

The two men I despised were sipping on what would only be the finest Russian vodka when I stepped into the room. They both turned in my direction, and I shuddered at the hunger I saw in Ivan's eyes.

"*Kraseevaia zhenshchina.*" *Beautiful woman*, Ivan murmured, and my nostrils flared angrily.

"Kira, come," the man who'd called himself my father ordered. As if I was a dog. Then again, I pretty much was now.

Gritting my teeth, I advanced to stand before them. Fists clenched, I was anything but demure.

"Time has been a good friend to you," Ivan said in heavily accented English as he fingered a loose strand of my hair. "I cannot wait to shove my dick in you until you scream."

"You want to fuck her now? As sign of good faith. Then we sign paperwork?" Grishka asked Ivan, whose eyes glinted greedily, and his tongue wet his lips. My heart raced, and my stomach revolted at the thought that Grishka would do that to me again.

"Bend over," Ivan instructed as he smiled evilly and motioned to the arm of the couch.

My eyes flickered around the room, hoping that someone would be around to stop what was about to happen. There wasn't a soul, though I had not a single doubt that my *father's* men were not far away.

"Fuck you," I spat.

"You think you have choice?" He chuckled darkly. "Do what I say, or I kill your mother, your filthy biker, your roommate, everyone you love. I will burn that piece of shit town in Iowa to the ground. I. Don't. Care."

Ivan advanced on me threateningly, and the knowledge that he would absolutely carry out his threat had me doing as he bid. The humiliation that washed over me was nearly suffocating. He teased his fingertips across my back, eliciting a shudder of revulsion that he happily mistook for desire. "You crave my touch, do you not, *malen'kaya ptitsa.*" *Little bird*, he crooned.

Then his hand grabbed my throat so hard I couldn't breathe. He jerked me upright and hissed in my ear, "What is this mark?"

Oh shit. I hadn't thought about the tattoo when I'd put my hair up. A frisson of fear made its way through me at what he might do. My mouth dry, I was unable to answer.

"What is this?" he screamed in my ear. "You allow another man to put his mark on you? I will burn it from your flesh until you know you are mine! Do you understand?"

He shook me by my neck, causing my hair to tumble free. A rampage of Russian spewed from his mouth as he shoved my face into the couch with my body bent over the arm. Though I thrashed and tried to fight him, he was a huge man, and I was no match for him.

My fighting seemed to amuse and excite him as he rubbed his hard dick against my ass. The cool air hit my skin as he jerked my dress over my hips. Tears trickled over my cheeks and into the couch when he ripped my panties away and tossed them.

I tried to kick back at him as I heard the clank of his belt. He knocked me upside my head for my efforts and held my head down. As I tasted blood from the reopened cut on my lip, I tried to clear my head. My gaze was blurred, but I could make out Grishka's form as he stood calmly drinking from his glass as he watched.

"I hate you!" I screamed, but unfazed, he simply let out a dark chuckle.

"You might want to wear a condom, Ivan. At least until you've had her tested. As I told you, her decisions of late have been poorly executed." Ivan snarled angrily and I knew in my heart that Grishka had only said that to enrage him. He wanted him to hurt me.

The painful invasion of Ivan's fingers had me crying out. But I twisted and fought with everything I had. He might take me, but I'd never be willing or compliant with him. Hell, if he killed me in anger, I'd be free of him quicker.

As he lined the tip of his dick up with my opening, I sobbed and frantically thrashed.

"Kalashnik, if you were a smart man, you'd call off your friend," I heard a familiar voice say from the other side of the couch. Ivan paused, which was followed by a shouted, "Now!"

One minute I was facedown on the couch. The next, I was in front of Ivan with his meaty hand around my neck and a knife held to my chin. It was ironic, considering that standing across the room was Shank, with my oldest brother held in a similar position.

Anatoly's eyes flashed defiantly as Shank jerked his head and pressed the knife in enough to draw blood. The dark trickle held me temporarily mesmerized.

Then my heart soared, because standing next to him, poised to launch, was Ogun. Except, the man standing there was not the sweet man who made love to me and laughed as we cooked dinner together.

No. That man was Voodoo. Eyes cold, body coiled, yet he barely moved a muscle as he held a wicked-looking gun pointed at Ivan.

Grishka growled. "You will regret this decision, biker trash."

"Yeah, I don't think it will be us that has regrets," Raptor said from the other side of Shank and my brother. His pistol was trained on the man I'd called my father.

After that, everything happened so fast, I couldn't be sure I caught it all.

Grishka pulled out a pistol of his own, one of his goons slipped around the corner behind, Voodoo and his brothers, then shots were fired, but I had no idea who fired first.

All I knew for certain was that poor Shank's face exploded outward from the blast of Grishka's man behind him, Voodoo grabbed my brother as Shank dropped to the ground, and the cold edge of Ivan's knife slid through my skin.

Shouts rang out everywhere, and I dropped to the cold marble tiles, unable to move. Footsteps running, a warm hand to my throat, and I choked. It took everything I had to blink as I stared up into the eyes of the man I loved.

"Angel!" he screamed. "Hurry!"

It was insane how fast things had moved with us, but I wanted to tell him I loved him more than life itself. Except my lips barely moved, and no sound would come out. Dizziness enveloped me, and the cold wrapped its icy tentacles around me, pulling me under.

So many regrets to die with.

SEVENTEEN

Voodoo

"SOMETHING LEFT TO SAVE"—DEADSET SOCIETY

She wasn't wearing white like in my visions and my dreams, but her thick crimson blood oozed between my fingers as I tried to stop the flow. Blood everywhere. Coating her chest, in her mouth. It matched the bloodred of her dress that ordinarily would've been beautiful on her.

"Voodoo, I need to see her before it's too late," Angel murmured as he laid a hand on my wrist. Confused and disoriented, I looked at him without moving. He nodded, and I dropped my gaze to my woman.

Swallowing the knot in my throat, I reluctantly set her on the floor. The puddle of blood under her seeped into the golden blonde hair that had been tangled around her head. Holding her lifeless hand in mine, I refused to let go.

My breathing came in shallow pants as I fought the rage that began to take over my broken heart. I prayed to God that she would make it, but if she didn't, I wouldn't rest until I'd stripped Ivan's flesh from his body, inch by inch.

"Shank?" I asked, but Angel shook his head desolately. There were limits to his ability.

"Voodoo, maybe you should go help Facet and Ghost. They are getting our guests secured, but we also need to load up Shank and clean up this mess." Raptor held a hand over his mouth as he looked down to where I sat on my ass, dazed and covered in Kira's blood.

"No. I'm not leaving her."

He gave me a look that said he wanted to chew my ass for refusing him, but I couldn't leave her like that, and he knew it. My gaze fell back on Angel where he was kneeling next to her still form. If anyone could save her, it was Angel. It gave me hope.

Raptor sighed. "Angel? You good?"

Angel looked up briefly and nodded, then returned his concentration to the broken love of my life in front of him. God, I sounded like a sappy fuck, but I loved her. So fucking much it hurt. Though I knew I'd move heaven and earth for her, I would also kill for her. And I intended to follow through on that when we were done in her father's penthouse.

Her father, her brother, Ivan—they'd all pay and pay dearly before I sent them to hell. If she died, I'd call Rael and Grim. I'd beg them to continue their torment on the way there. See, there were things about some of the chapters of our club that not everyone knew.

Little whispers.

Rumors that held more truth than they realized.

Yet they had no idea the extent of the things some of our chapters consisted of. Not really.

The faint glow that filled the space between Angel's hands

and Kira's body was mesmerizing. Slowly, I watched as the blood stopped seeping out of the gaping wound on her neck.

From the inside out, her tissue closed, achingly slowly. Finally, the surface of her skin slowly folded together, sealing itself as if it hadn't been gaping open mere seconds ago. The blood was drying on her skin, but other than a faint scar, the cut was as if it had never happened.

Still, she lay lifeless. I stared and willed her to open her eyes. Scanning her from head to toe, I waited for a movement. With closed eyes, Angel moved his hands to her head, and they hovered over the swollen and bruised area that had hit the floor after Ivan slit her throat.

When he was done, he dropped his head in exhaustion. Silently, I watched him, knowing how what he'd done depleted him. Gratitude filled me at his sacrifice.

"Angel?" I asked, afraid to voice the rest of my thoughts. She still hadn't moved, but an extremely faint pulse flickered beneath my fingertip that rested on her wrist.

"I've done all I can, Voodoo. She lost a lot of blood. Ideally, she should have a transfusion. If we were at home, I have contacts. But here? We'll have to wait." The bleakness in his gaze ripped my heart out. He didn't have to say that he was skeptical; I could read it in his eyes.

Loath to let go of her but knowing he was on the verge of collapse, I reverently set her hand to the floor and lifted my brother to his feet. Shuffling with him, I helped him to the couch. He sat heavily and fell to his side. After lifting his feet, I rested a hand on his shoulder.

"Can I get you anything?"

He shook his head and closed his eyes. We'd grown up together, and he was more than my brother in the club. He was my friend, my confidant, my brother in my heart to the extent that I'd followed him into the army even thought I knew we'd both end up back in Ankeny as brothers in the Royal Bastards.

I'd needed to be there to protect him from his self-destructive nature at the time. He'd always been a contradiction. It amazed me that the man known as the Angel of Death for our chapter was blessed with the ability to save lives as well as take them.

"Rest, brother. We'll need to leave soon."

When I was certain he was resting comfortably, I returned to Kira. It might've been my imagination, but it seemed like her pulse was stronger, and the faint movement of her chest was noticeable.

Carefully, I lifted her from the floor and brought her to the first bedroom I came upon. Once I set her on the bed, I pulled the blanket up from the other side and covered her with it.

Crouching next to her, I gently pulled the hair loose from where it was stuck to her skin with dried blood. The thought of her not being in my life was something I didn't want to contemplate.

"You need to pull through, baby. Sasha is waiting for you at home, and I don't want to have to tell her I couldn't bring you back. You hear me?" I sucked in a shaky inhale. "And I don't want to imagine life without you. I finally got you; I'm not ready to let you go."

I pressed a kiss on her forehead and pushed my emotions to the back of my mind. Moving on autopilot, I searched the penthouse for the supplies I needed. I'd set the last item next to the mess in the living room when Facet, Ghost, and Raptor returned.

The space where Shank's body had been was eerily cold, and I knew we all experienced it. They had rolled his body up in the area rug he'd fallen on and had dragged him back to the elevator area to wait for us. We'd bring him home to his ol' lady and give him the sendoff he deserved as a loyal long-term Bastard.

Quietly and efficiently, we erased all signs that the night's events had taken place. It was, after all, our specialty. Our cleaning company did this professionally, so it was damn near second nature for us and came in handy after situations like we'd found ourselves in.

"How is she?" Ghost asked as we bagged up the last of the cleaning items and the clothes we'd been wearing. It would all be incinerated.

None of us cared that we were standing there in our underwear. Facet had gone down to the parking garage to retrieve our change of clothes from our bikes. He'd bypassed the security system, leaving everything on a loop since before we pulled into the garage. No one would be the wiser that we'd been there. Especially since all the witnesses were either dead or coming back with us.

It would be tricky crossing state lines in an out-of-state SUV with several bodies in a trailer we'd rented to carry Angel's bike. We'd decided he would drive one of Kalashnik's SUVs in case Kira needed him. It set my teeth on edge, because I wanted to be with her.

"Voodoo," Facet said as he tossed me my bag. I caught it midair and returned to the room Kira rested in. I'd been in to check on her several times while we cleaned, but there hadn't been a change.

Quickly, I dressed as I kept an eye on her.

While I waited for my brothers, I went into the bathroom

and grabbed several towels and wet a few washcloths. Carefully, I cleaned as much of the blood from her as I could, disposing of the towels in a bag and tying it off.

"Ready?" Raptor asked from the doorway. I nodded. "Okay, wrap her in the comforter. Bring any of the linens that she's touched or bloodied. Ghost and Facet are going to do a final wipe-down before we lock the place up."

"I know what I'm doing," I grumbled at his lack of faith in my ability not to leave behind evidence.

"Hey. It wasn't anything personal. I just know you might not be thinking clearly."

"I'm good. Kalashnik still alive?" I asked.

He nodded. "Both of them. For now. Grishka might not make it back to Ankeny, but we'll see."

"I want him alive." My teeth ground in frustration.

"Voodoo. I'm not going to drain Angel again by having him treat that Russian piece of shit just so you can torture him." His exasperation did nothing for me.

"It's my right!" I roared as I took heaving breaths. The windows shuddered. A glass vase shook on the dresser and toppled over. Raptor snagged it before it hit the floor.

"Chill, bro. We don't have time to clean more messes."

Clenching my fists, I nodded. Yeah, I knew he was right, but it didn't help.

The trip back to Ankeny seemed to take twice as long, since we didn't dare ride like we had on the way there. There was too much to lose if we got pulled over. We'd even secured our cuts in our saddlebags so we wouldn't stand out to any of the locals. If anyone saw our Iowa plates, we were nothing more than a group of civilians on our way home from a road trip.

During our last gas stop, I checked on Kira again. We had lain all the back seats down, made a bed with her head up by Angel, and strapped her down the best we could. Each stop had been the same.

No change.

Except during the last one, she didn't seem quite as pale. While the brothers stretched their legs and checked on our "cargo," I climbed in to sit next to her. Though she was still unconscious, I talked to her like she could hear me.

"We're almost home, baby. I swear to fuck, you better wake up. I've gone almost thirty years without you, and I'm not prepared to do any more. You hear me? We have puppies to raise. We have vows to say. We have babies to make. In fact, I might plant a baby in you before the vows just to make sure you don't try to go anywhere." A sad smile curled the corner of my lips as I imagined her swatting at me and telling me I was crazy. More than anything, I wanted her to open her eyes and tell me I was a misogynistic asshole.

Not that I really was. I'd never believed in that barefoot and pregnant shit.

Hell, we had a fucking female president in the Baltimore chapter. Granted, we'd been pissed as fuck at Ghost for stepping in to help her, but I'd had time to reconsider. The older brothers of our chapter would never allow a woman to be voted in as a member, but it didn't mean I didn't respect Gamble and the shit she went through.

"You're supposed to tell me to fuck off, then I tell you to make me, then I fuck you compliant."

"Wow, you're a real romantic. How ever does she resist you?" My head swiveled to Ghost standing in the partially open door.

"Jesus fucking Christ, bro! That shit isn't funny." He'd damn near gotten his nose caved in.

Completely nonplussed, he shrugged and grinned. "Just thought you might like to know that Angel did you a little favor."

"Little?" I motioned to Kira. "I'd say it was huge." Though she hadn't woken up yet, at least she was still alive. For now.

"Wasn't referring to her." He gave a smirk, a lift of his chin, and walked off toward the bikes.

Brow furrowed, I watched him go. It wasn't long before Angel made his way back to the vehicle. He had his arms full of a giant drink, a bag of licorice, one of those long beef sticks, some chips, and a banana.

"Goddamn, bro. Hungry much?" My eyes bugged at all the junk food he carried.

"I needed to build my strength back up." He lifted a shoulder and popped a piece of licorice in his mouth. As he chewed, I shot him a look that clearly stated *What the actual fuck?* and shook my head in amazement.

"What was Ghost talking about when he said you did me a little favor?"

He pursed his lips, looked off to the side, and took a long pull from his drink.

"Angel," I said in warning. He darted his gaze back to me, then bit his lip as he juggled his shit and put it in the SUV.

"I may have done enough to keep that dick-gargling fucklord alive for you for a bit," he said in a low voice.

"What the fuck did you just say?"

"Dick-gargling fucklord. I saw it on my social media the other day." Shrugging, he peeked in at Kira. He checked her pulse and sighed.

Despite the seriousness of our situation, I laughed. "You're not all there. You know that, right?"

He shot me a huge smile and wiggled his brows. "I know, right?"

"Thanks, bro. For everything." I experienced a moment of humble emotion. He grinned and climbed in the driver seat. Twisting slightly in his seat, he trailed his fingertips over Kira's forehead.

"I'm worried," I said as I held her hand.

"Let's get on the road." His answer wasn't reassuring in the least. If I was honest with myself, I was terrified to let go of her in case the next time we stopped she was gone. Reluctantly, I kissed her head, then the back of her hand.

We got back on the road, and my mind was a mess. So much so, I was glad I'd been with my brothers, because I didn't remember the last of the miles passing. I'd have rather taken her home, but I knew why we went directly to the clubhouse.

"Get her in the infirmary." The gruff voice of Doc shocked me. I hadn't expected him to be there.

Sensing my surprise, Angel squeezed my shoulder, and I carried Kira's limp body to the room in the back we'd designated as an infirmary. My steps stuttered as I stepped through and saw it set up like the best of hospital rooms, complete with infusion setup.

"I called ahead," Angel said with a small smile. My heart ached at his foresight, and I'd never been more thankful for him. Last I heard, Doc had all but moved down by the border to Missouri to be closer to his grandkids.

"Thanks, Doc." I fought choking up. He had very similar abilities to Angel, but he'd actually been a doctor in the army, and then an ER doctor before he'd completely retired.

Once I had her situated, he wasted no time in getting IV access established and pulled blood products from the cooler. "How the fuck did you know her blood type?"

Angel gave me a smug grin. Facet stepped into the doorway and cleared his throat. "Well, before we left Chicago, Angel asked me to hack into her medical records to find out her blood type."

"We could've went with an O negative, but since we were able to get access, I was able to hook her up with her specific blood type. Which was good, because O negative isn't always easy to get ahold of on the sly," Doc explained as he got everything running, took vitals, and watched everything that was happening. His hands may have been weathered and aged, but he moved confidently.

Angel assisted him as needed and gently moved me out of the way to sit up by Kira's head.

"We don't know exactly how much blood she lost or how much she needs, so I'm going to have to see if between Angel and I, we can sense when we're good. Then we wait," he finished as he looked up at me.

"Thank you. Both of you."

"Voodoo. Prez wants to see you for a second," Raptor said from out in the hall.

Sensing my hesitation, Angel and Doc both motioned for me to go. Raptor rested a hand on my shoulder. "She's in good hands, brother. It won't take long."

Rushing so I could get back, I stepped into Venom's office. He was finishing up on the phone and looked at me as he hung up. "That was Ghost. He, Squirrel, and Blade have our guests situated. Thought you might like to know something Squirrel got out of the son."

One brow shot up as I waited. Venom stared at me for some time, as if he was trying to gauge how pissed I was going to be.

"Kalashnik paid a member of the Bloody Scorpions to nab Kira."

"What? Why? Couldn't he have sent one of his own men to get her?" The Bloody Scorpions were the worst of the worst. You name it, they were into it. Everything from meth and heroin to human trafficking. Seriously fucked-up shit. It was also the club in which my biological father had been a member. If he was still alive like my grandmother believed, then he likely still was. But why would he be here now?

"Maybe. We think it's because there was more to the deal. You need to be careful. Something tells me it's no coincidence that they're involved. Top it off with all the times you've sensed you're being watched, and I don't fucking like it. Anyway, the assholes in the slaughterhouse aren't going anywhere, but I wanted you to know we don't have much time. De Luca expects you to uphold your end of the bargain."

"Don't worry. Tell him we have them. Send him proof if you need to. But tell him I get my time first. Then I'll do as he wants. Facet was already on the Ivan situation. Most of his money is about to be liquidated." I gave an evil grin at the thought of the New York City bratva leader being destitute and unable to pay his minions. It was a toss-up as to whether the better revenge was killing him or having him face his crew without any money.

"Raptor filled me in on everything that went down in Chicago. Are you sure your head's in the right place to deal with all this?" He studied me intently, waiting for my reaction.

Inhaling a slow, deep breath, I took my time exhaling. "I've got this. Anything else?"

For a few seconds he steadily held my gaze. "No."

Getting up, I paused. "Thanks for allowing me to handle this my way." He nodded, and I left.

Ghost caught me in the hall. "Brother, I'm sorry."

"Stop. I already told you, it wasn't your fault."

"If I'd gotten to him quicker—"

"No. We can't control everything, nor can we manipulate everything the way we want it. We can only do our best—and that's what we did. You had no way of knowing it was Ivan you needed to go after instead of Kalashnik. Thankfully, Angel was there."

"I know, but she still hasn't woken up." His brow furrowed, and he looked away.

"I believe she's going to be okay," I reassured him.

"Do you?" His eyes flashed back to mine, almost in challenge.

"I do."

Our gazes held for a moment, then he dropped his and nodded. My hand gripped his shoulder firmly, then I released him and continued on.

As I passed my room, I made a quick detour. Closing my door, I stepped inside, opened the closet, and pushed the few clothes from the middle to the sides. Kneeling down, I said a quick prayer, lit my sage and herb mixture, and picked up my *gris gris* bag. Holding a hand over my worn cards, I prayed to decide which to use.

I left the cards.

After untying the worn leather tie, I prayed again. Several times, I pulled an item from the bag and set it on the worn piece of red flannel. Studying them, I selected a few of them, returning the remaining to my bag and setting it to the side.

My fingers trailed over the various objects that sat on the small upper shelf, and I selected several small stones—two smooth, one rough. They went on the flannel cloth as well.

Next, I grabbed my bones from the scarred wooden bowl on the shelf and threw them. Scrying was a more challenging method, but I seemed to get more accurate answers when I did it.

Selecting several that called to me, I arranged them and waited. Then I took the remainder, threw them again, selected more, and repeated the process. Finally, I scooped up the bones left on the table, raised them, then dropped them to the table.

Stopping to read them, I chanted low and breathed in the smoke. Then I returned them all to the soft bag and cleared my head as I rewrapped my *gris gris* bag.

Taking a strip of leather, I wrapped the flannel around the items that had been selected and secured it. As I chanted under my breath, I waved the small red pouch over the smoke. When I was done, I tucked them both in my pocket and extinguished the sage.

Once I knew everything was safe, I returned the closet to the way it was, and closed the doors.

Then I returned to Kira.

The blood had run, and Doc was putting everything away. Angel sat in a chair at the foot of the bed with his head bowed. Slipping past them, I pulled the other chair up next to her and tucked the red cloth pouch into the soft curl of her hand.

Holding it against her skin, I bowed my head and prayed. Never ceasing, I chanted the prayer my grandmother had taught me as a young boy.

I had no idea how long I'd been there before I fell asleep, my head lying on the bed next to her still, but thankfully warm, hand.

EIGHTEEN

Kira

"DAWN WILL RISE"—THIRTY SECONDS TO MARS

I'd been fighting through the heavy fog for what seemed like hours. Over and over, I stumbled and fell. Nothing made sense. I would come across people, but they seemed to stare through me no matter how much I begged them to look at me.

Because there was very little light and no landmarks, I had no idea if I was going in circles, but I came across the same older woman time and time again. Her mouth would move, but no sound would ever come out.

I'd screamed for Ogun repeatedly until I was hoarse.

It wasn't until I begged for him as Voodoo that the fog began to thin. Through the wisps, I saw his tall, imposing, and beautiful form emerging. My heart racing, I ran.

When I slammed into his broad chest and his arms wrapped around me, I cried tears of joy. He looked down at me and his mouth curled into a beautiful smile. Relief poured through me as I reached up to press my lips to his—except right as they brushed his, he faded into smoke and was gone.

Spinning around, I screamed for him. When I realized he was truly gone, I dropped to my knees, sobbing. It was then that I realized there was something in my hand, but I didn't remember him giving anything to me.

Slowly, I unfolded my fingers to find a velvety-soft red flannel pouch.

The next thing I remembered was fighting to open my eyes. My lids were so weighted that it was a struggle, but finally, I blinked weakly. Everything in me ached. Trying to move proved impossible. I was as weak as a newborn.

With each breath I took, it seemed I inhaled more life. Sensing movement, I lifted my head from the pillow. Standing in the corner, watching me intently, was Ghost.

"Ghost?" Confused, I questioned him. He gave me a half smile, then I swear to fucking Christ, he disappeared before my eyes. "What the—"

Then I realized Ogun was asleep next to me. Well, he was sitting in a chair that looked uncomfortable as hell, his dark head resting next to my hand. When I made a move to reach for him, my hand slowly opened, and the red pouch from my dream was in it.

My brow furrowed as I stared at it in confusion.

Passing it to my other hand, I squeezed it tight and sifted my free hand through his dark, messy hair. My thumb traced over the arch of his bold brow. Slowly, his eyes opened, and the startling blue took my breath away.

It seemed an eternity, but I knew it was mere heartbeats that we sat with gazes locked before he bolted upright.

"Kira," he rasped in a sleep-scratchy tone. His expression

eager, he tenderly kissed the inside of my wrist. "How are you feeling?"

"Confused. Tired. Weak." Glancing around, I furrowed my forehead. "Where are we? What happened? And what is this?" I held up the small red pouch.

"Fuck, baby. So much." Carefully, he scooted me over in the bed and crawled in with me. Then he tucked me into his warmth, and everything was perfect. A sigh of satisfaction slipped from my soul. "That is a *gris gris* I made for you. Keep it with you always, okay?"

"Why? What's in it?" Holding it up, I felt several small objects inside it.

"Little bits of things that have energy or protective properties that I read for you" was his vague answer. Then he kissed me so softly, it was a mere feather of a touch, yet it still made me forget where my head had been.

I think I dozed again, but I had no idea for how long. When I woke, I was tightly entwined with Ogun, and his thick, strong arm held me protectively as he lightly snored. A smile curled my lips as I burrowed deeper into his embrace.

"You awake?" he murmured against the top of my head.

"Yeah, but I had the weirdest dream earlier," I whispered. His chest rumbled under me as he chuckled, then his hands gently framed my face and lifted my head. His eyes searched mine, then he met me halfway and our lips brushed.

Flames licked at the edges of my sanity. Crawling up his massive body, I leaned over him and allowed my hair to curtain us. Desire rippled through my veins, and I couldn't get enough of him.

Reluctantly, he broke free and lifted me back. Our gasping breaths still mingled, and I arched into him with a moan.

"Easy, I don't want you to overdo things."

"I don't know what you mean," I said as I tried to get back to his kisses. Again, he chuckled.

"My little wild one," he said with a soft half smile.

"I love you, Ogun," I blurted out, unable to hold it in anymore. It was as though if I didn't get it out that very second, I may never have the chance to say it again.

His chest lifted as he sucked in a breath, then it deflated quickly. "Fuck, babe. I love you too. Probably have from the first second I laid eyes on you."

My heart imploded with joy. Then my body rubbed greedily against his, but he stilled my motions.

"Wait. Let me have Doc check you out. Okay?"

"Doc?" I wrinkled my nose. Dr. Moran was *not* going to be assessing me! Petulant, I grunted. He lifted his hips to pull out his phone. He sent a text, then set the phone down. "Come here. Let me hold you."

Unable to resist, I settled into him and rested there until the door opened and he carefully extricated himself from me and got out of the bed. An older guy I assumed was the Doc Ogun had been referring to stepped into the room. A kind smile went all the way to his eyes.

"Hello, Kira. I'm Doc. You gave us quite a scare. Do you mind if I do a quick exam?"

My eyes darted to Ogun, begging him not to leave me. "I'm naked," I whispered with wide eyes.

"That big oaf can stay in here if you want," Doc said with a chuckle. An embarrassed smile slipped across my face as I nodded.

Ogun pressed a kiss to the top of my head.

Doc did all the typical things a doctor does. Stethoscope,

light in my eyes, feeling my lymph nodes and all that shit. But then he skimmed his hands over me as his eyes remained closed. Though I could feel the heat from his palms, he didn't actually make contact with me.

When he was done, his eyes opened and he seemed extremely pleased.

"Good?" Ogun asked.

"Perfect," Doc replied.

Ogun exhaled a sigh of profound relief. Then he shot off another text before raising his gaze to me and Doc.

"I'm taking her to my room to get cleaned up. I told Venom I'd be back tonight to finish up."

Doc nodded and returned his attention to me. "It was a pleasure meeting you—the one who finally tamed this young scoundrel. Wish it had been under better circumstances, but we don't always choose our paths." He looked toward Ogun. "If there's nothing else you need, I'm heading back to my grandbabies."

Ogun reached out to shake his hand, then pulled him into a weird handshake/hug thing. They whispered a few things, and Doc stepped back with a wry grin.

"Take care of this one," he said to me. "I already know he'll take good care of you." With one last nod, he was gone.

"Ogun. What the fuck was that?" I asked in consternation. It was honestly as if I'd dropped into someone else's life. In another dimension.

Instead of answering me, he dragged a hand through his dark locks and down his face.

"Come on, baby, let's get you cleaned up." He picked me up like a child and carried me down the hall wrapped in the white sheet and into the room I remembered very well from our first date.

When he set me on my feet in the bathroom, he rested my ass against the edge of the sink. "Lean on there for balance."

"I'm fine." I waved off his fussing hands. "What the hell is going on?"

When I tried to turn to the mirror, he stopped me. "Get in the shower," he urged. My eyes narrowed. He was acting weird. Thinking about it, I realized something, and before he could stop me, I spun around.

The image in the mirror had me gasping in horror. Someone had obviously tried to clean me up, but there was still blood crusted in my hair, smeared across my chest, on my arms. It was like I'd been part of a sick movie or killed an animal. Or worse.

The sheet dropped forgotten to the floor as I looked again for some sign of injury.

Because other than being a little weak, I was fine. The entire scan of myself in the mirror and looking down at my body showed nothing. Not a scratch. Whipping around, I started to strip his clothes off him in a frantic rush. He stilled my hands when I got to the waistband of his jeans.

"Kira." When I fought to finish undressing him, he said my name more forcefully. "Kira!"

Finally, I paused. A shaking breath dragged deep into my lungs, and I slowly met his eyes. "Are you hurt?"

"No." He seemed to be waiting for something.

"What the hell happened? Ogun, this is getting weird. Talk to me. I know you know something." The whole this was giving me a headache.

"How about if we get you cleaned up first?"

"No. Now," I demanded as my head pounded.

Looking skyward, he seemed to be trying to find the words. What he finally told me was a story so unreal that I seriously believed I was dreaming. The thought that people could "magically" *heal* someone on their deathbed was something from fairy tales and movies.

"Then why don't I remember any of this?" I skeptically questioned. My mind went crazy trying to remember. Except I had no idea how I'd ended up in that bed, or why I was covered in dried blood. The last thing I remembered was walking out the door after work.

"I don't have an answer for that," he replied. "Maybe it was your mind's way of protecting you from a breakdown? Fuck, I have no clue."

"What if I don't believe you?" Lifting my chin, I crossed my arms and stared at him. My eyes squinted as I fought the raging pain.

"To be honest, I don't expect you to, but that's what happened. What you shouldn't know, but you have a right to know, is that your father isn't going to survive this. Neither is your brother." His nostrils flared, and I read blazing anger in his eyes.

"My brother?" My heart dropped at the thought of Viktor or Dmitry being in danger. My father, I could care less about, because since I was fifteen and he ruined me, I'd fought to keep the utter hatred I had for him bottled up.

With a curl of his lip, he spat, "Anatoly."

Relief blossomed in me, because Anatoly was as evil as our father. "Fine. But why are you telling me this if you aren't supposed to?"

"Because there are things that we do as Royal Bastards that you don't need to know about. There will be many things that will fall under club business that I won't be able to tell you, but this is your family we're talking about."

At the word family, I clutched my head—the pain

excruciating by then. It was so bad, I cried out and nearly collapsed.

Ogun's hands were holding me up, and I could hear him calling out to me, then someone else. Except it was but a mumble over the whooshing in my head. Flashes of images bombarded me and with them, the past twenty-four hours flooded back.

Pushing free of his hold, I leaned over the toilet and emptied my stomach. The sheet was draped over me, and I looked up to find it was Ogun covering me as Angel stepped into the small space.

"Get your big ass out of the way," Angel said to Ogun, who growled at him.

Angel laid a calloused palm against my cheek and the other at the back of my head. Slowly, the pain began to ease, but the tears still ran down my face. "Breathe easy, little one," he murmured.

"So you really saved me?" I asked in confusion, because I was completely and totally overwhelmed by that point.

Of course, he didn't answer, merely shrugged modestly. He was a hard man to read.

"Can you take your hands off my woman now?" Ogun growled. Angel chuckled, winked at me, then released my face.

"Let me know if you need anything else," he said before he kissed the top of my head and stood, drawing another growl out of Ogun. It was pretty evident he'd done that to mess with him.

"Sasha?" I questioned, dread pooling in my belly.

"She's gonna be okay. She's with Veronica, as she needed to be monitored overnight. I'm paying her to keep her for a couple of days because I wasn't sure how your recovery would go," Ogun said softly. Relief had me sagging into the wall.

They spoke quietly over by the door to the room while I

got up and turned on the water for the shower. They were still talking by the time the water got warm, so I stepped under the spray. Closing my eyes, I let the water beat down on me as I replayed the events of the past twenty-four hours—hell, I wasn't sure what time it was, so I didn't know how long it had been.

"Got room in there for me?" My head rose at the sexy rasp of his voice over the shower. As beads of water dripped from my eyelashes, I nodded. Slowly, he climbed in and turned me around. My shoulders drooped as he massaged shampoo into my hair and scalp.

When he was done, he gently tugged my head back and rinsed it. A soft kiss was pressed to the pulse in my neck where I knew I should have a scar. Then he reverently lathered my body, all the way down to my feet.

Each stroke of his hands over my skin, brush of his lips, scrape of his teeth, was nothing less than worship. "I love you," he whispered in my ear before he held my hair to the side and kissed my nape where my tattoo started.

A shiver skated through me at the sensuousness of his touch and the emotions it elicited.

I sucked in a startled breath when his tongue traced the lines of the tattoo.

"What does this say?" he asked.

"You know," I gasped. His teeth sank into the corded muscles at the slope of my shoulder.

"Say it," he demanded before he sucked on the side of my neck. Chills hit me, and I arched into him with need. The hard length of his cock slid through the crease of my ass.

When I tried to tip my hips to bring him between my legs, he pulled back. "Say. It," he bit out with a growl in my ear and a tweak to each nipple before he settled on one.

Whimpering with need, I reached back to grab him and panted out what he wanted to hear.

"I'm yours."

"Goddamn right you are," he said with a feral groan. His arms were wrapped around me. One held the column of my throat as he teased the side of my neck. The other went from torturing my nipples to circling my clit. I fought between trying to increase the pressure to my clit and pressing back into his cock.

"Ogun, I need you. Please," I begged.

"Not yet," he murmured as he continued to play with me. By the time his fingers slid between my pussy lips, I was damn near writhing with desire. Lust exploded in my chest and flooded every inch of me. A dark chuckle sounded as he thrust in the slick crease repeatedly.

Two fingers, then three filled me as the heel of his hand ground against my clit and he continued to stroke against my ass. "Please," I cried as I rode his hand like I was having a fucking seizure.

Steadily, he worked me over until I threw my head back as I shouted his name. The pulsing of his cock against my ass and the hot burst to my back were followed by his moans against the wet skin of my shoulder.

Legs like Jell-O, I could barely stand. He rinsed us off with rapidly cooling water, then shut it off and opened the shower door. He stepped out first and grabbed two towels. One he used to dry every inch of me before wrapping my hair up. The other, dried himself with as I watched hungrily.

"Just because you made me come, doesn't mean I don't still want you inside me," I said in a husky tone. It made me feel powerful to watch his cock jump at my words.

"I don't want to overtax you. You've been through a lot."

Weak rationale. I felt incredible—all things considered.

Without arguing, I gathered my courage and walked naked to his bed. Taking my time, I arched my back invitingly as I turned the linens back. The sharp inhalation told me that he'd gotten an eyeful when I'd bent over.

A naughty smile curled my lips as I shed the towel from my hair and climbed into the bed. My gaze caught and held his as I bent my legs up and spread them wide. With one hand, I played with my nipple like he had in the shower; the other slipped between my legs.

"I want you," I said before sliding two fingers deep inside my heated channel and running my tongue over my bottom lip. Greedily, my pussy gripped my fingers like I wanted to do to his thick cock. "Here."

"Goddamn motherfuckin' temptress," he muttered as he stalked to the bed. He stopped at the foot, staring at where my fingers made slick, sloppy sounds as they slid in and out. My heart began to race in anticipation, and my chest heaved as I tried to drag oxygen into my lungs. The thought of having him inside me was enough to kick up all my body's systems until I thought I might combust.

With a growl, he grabbed my ankles and jerked me down until my ass almost fell off the bed, the comforter rolled and wadded underneath me. As I gripped his cock tight and stroked it until a clear bead of precum dripped from the tip, the messed-up covers no longer mattered. Then he lined it up and shoved that fucker all the way to the base.

Though I was prepared, I screamed his name at the perfect blend of pleasure and pain. He pushed my ankles until my knees were to my chest. "That's what you get for teasing," he ground out as he smacked my ass. My eyes bugged in surprise, but the wetness that flooded my pussy was what shocked me more than his hand landing on my tender flesh.

Without giving me time to adjust, he pulled back his hips and thrust forward. Harder and harder he fucked me, sending my eyes closed, a grunt escaping my lips with each deep thrust. Every so often, he would give me a smack to one side or the other. By then my ass was burning and tender, but I was in sensation overload, teetering on falling off the ledge.

"Jesus fucking Christ, you feel so good. So fucking good," he ground out as he plowed into me again and again. His fingertips dug into the front of my thighs for better grip. I'd surely have bruises, but I didn't care. All that mattered was us and how good we were together.

Sex with Ogun was dark and dangerous, yet everything good, all wrapped up into one tempting ball of sin. One that I'd happily jump on the bus to hell for in order to experience it for the rest of my life.

"Fuck! Oh God! I'm going to come!" I burst out as it hit me like a freaking truck. I was thrashing, and my eyes rolled in my head as he continued to fuck me through the mind-altering orgasm of the century.

"Yes! Fuuuuck!" He moaned as he buried himself deep, and the powerful pulsing of his thick cock told me he was filling me with his hot cum. That alone sent me into cataclysmic aftershocks of my orgasm. Hell, it might've been another one altogether. I'd honestly lost track.

When my head finally quit spinning and I was capable of speech, I stared, dazed, at the ceiling.

"Fuck, I think my hooha might be broken after that," I said as I damn near drooled in my sexually satisfied stupor.

His gasping bark of laughter caused him to slip out a little.

As he leaned up between my legs, he pushed his semihard length inside again and kissed me. "I'd be willing to bet you anything you wanted that it's just fine. If you give me a bit to recover, I'll prove it to you."

That caused me to laugh, and it pushed him out all the way. We both groaned in disappointment, and my nose curled at the warmth running out of me because I knew it was landing on the covers.

He helped my boneless body up the bed, then crawled up to wrap around me like a giant man-cocoon. Those skilled fingers of his trailed across my skin, and a comfortable silence ensued.

Finally, I asked the question that had been in the back of my mind. "What are you going to do with Grishka and Anatoly?"

"I can't say more than I already have. But what I can tell you is that you need never fear them again." It was said with such finality that I knew he meant what he'd said earlier—that they were going to die. Deep inside, I tried to find empathy or sorrow, but I couldn't. Not a scrap.

Unable to respond, I nodded.

Little did he know, I had a plan of my own.

NINETEEN

Voodoo

"VOODOO II"—GODSMACK

By the time we'd made it back to Ankeny, it had been early afternoon. Then we'd had Kira to take care of. The plan had been to deal with Kira's father, brother, and Ivan that night, but Venom decided it wouldn't hurt to let them stew in their own piss and shit for a day. Literally.

I'd taken advantage of the unexpected free night to fuck Kira six ways from Sunday. We had dozed in between, but for most of the night and day after we'd returned, I'd been buried balls deep in her.

The decision to tell her what had happened hadn't been made lightly. I'd debated heavily. In the end, the fact that I loved her, she was mine, and I wasn't letting her go pretty much sealed the deal. If she was going to be around, she was going to find out a lot of things eventually.

She'd taken it better than I'd thought, but I still didn't think she believed half of it.

After a particularly intense fuck session, I'd left her sleeping to get dressed. She was worn the fuck out.

"I'll be back in a bit," I said softly as I kissed her naked shoulder. The sheet rode low, exposing the sexy curve of her lower back and her bared shoulders as she lay on her stomach in my bed. With her hair swept to the side and my brand showing on her neck, a mixture of lust, pride, and caveman-like possession rushed through me. My next kiss was on the center of her ink.

"Mmm. Promise?" she murmured sleepily. One hazel eye peeked up at me as the corner of her lips lifted. It sent a flutter through my chest and ended with me having to adjust my junk.

She lifted her head when she saw I was fully dressed. Suddenly wide awake, she furrowed her brow. "Where are you going?"

Raised up like she was, the tops of her perfect tits were calling to me. It happened every time. Kira was a distraction that more often than not had me wanting to throw everything by the wayside and climb in bed with her forever. It was a foreign concept for me. Before her, I'd never been romantic, emotional, or ruled by my dick.

"Club business to deal with" was my vague answer, but I saw the wheels turning and could damn near visualize her putting everything together. "I gotta go."

"Wait! I want to go with you!" She jumped up and started pulling clothes on. She'd hooked her bra backwards the way women did and spun it around to flip it over her tits before I could open my mouth.

"Kira. No. I need you to wait here," I insisted. She paused, and I kissed her. Then I took advantage of her half-naked state—that I really wanted to explore further—and left the room in a hurry.

Chains, Ghost, and Angel were waiting for me out in the common area. "Everyone already there?" Ghost nodded. There was a prospect at the bar, and I called out to him. "Prospect! No one goes in and out but a patched member. You feel me?"

"Got it," he replied with a firm nod. Then he continued stocking the bar in preparation for tomorrow night's party. After the week we'd had, everyone needed to blow off some steam. There would be an official church, then the party would start.

"Let's roll," I said to my brothers. They followed behind me. As the senior enforcer, I'd temporarily been promoted to SAA. It churned my gut that I'd stepped up into the position because Shank had died, but it was the way of our world.

We stepped out into the dark night, and the sound of crickets echoed into the night. Instead of getting on our bikes and riding down the road, we'd decided to take the path. At the back of the clubhouse property was a place where the lilac bushes could be pushed to the side, and it opened to a path that ran between the fields and went over to the hog farm.

It was maybe a mile or two walk, but it was less conspicuous than a bunch of bikes riding up into the hog farm at that time of night. We walked in a single file line through the break in the crops. No one said a word.

The glow around the buildings was our beacon as we trudged over. Once we got there, I broke off and went into my sanctuary.

After a brief prayer, I prepared what I needed and placed it in a softly worn leather satchel. Meticulously, I painted my face in white and black. When I was satisfied with my work, I gathered my things and stepped outside.

The walk from my shed to where I met everyone in the old slaughterhouse was short, but I paused when I thought I heard something. A scan of the area showed no movement in the dark shadows created by the full moon. Satisfied, I continued on.

"Voodoo, something's not right," Ghost said as he appeared next to me. That time, I'd sensed his presence, so the fucker didn't get the better of me. Pausing with the door opened partially, I met his gaze.

"You heard it too?" I was referring to the sound I'd heard. He shook his head. "Then what?"

"I'm not sure. Lots of whispers that I can't make out. Something has stirred up the spirits. I don't fucking like it." The hogs in the nearest building were also restless. Usually by this time of night they were bedded down and sleeping.

"Anyone else sense anything?" I asked as I took another sweep of the landscape.

"No."

"Maybe it's just the moon," I offered. He shrugged. "Stay alert. Let's go in. I'm anxious to get started."

Together, we slipped in the door and entered the old building. We followed the entry hall, and around the corner everyone was gathered around the three men we had hanging from the meat hooks by chains. Their arms were stretched above their heads, and their toes barely touched the floor. They'd been stripped naked.

Squirrel had rigged up an ingenious contraption that made me chuckle inside. Each of the three men had the end of a big fat dildo shoved up their asses. The dildos were attached to a frame that was attached to the floor, utilizing the eye-bolts we chained people to on the ground. If they pulled back at all, it would shove it farther up their butts.

If they were into that and it didn't bother them, then Phoenix was ready to deal with them.

When I stepped out of the shadows, I knew my face paint had startled them, and it gave me great satisfaction. Ivan's eyes were wary. The other two were still both defiant. I didn't care.

Slowly, I walked around the room, lighting the candles on the floor. The stench from their excrement was already acrid. The damp floor told me they'd already been hosed off at least once, with everything running down the drain in the center of the room.

When I stopped in front of them, I set up an altar. A silver bowl and a small, sheathed razor-sharp blade were the first items I brought out of the satchel. Then the rest of the items were set on the altar as I arranged everything the way I wanted it. Pulling my piece from the holster at my side, I set it on the table too. Specific candles were lit for the altar. Finally, I removed the ornate scabbard. The surgically sharp blade slid out with a metallic zing.

"What's with this freak?" Kalashnik spat. "You think you scare us with this Halloween charade?"

I allowed a slight smile to move my lips as I otherwise ignored them. He came across as brave, but I'd seen the sheen of sweat over his upper lip and brow. The blood from his gunshot wound was dried on him, but the opening was mostly healed closed.

I knew that had been Angel's work, and my eyes sought him out in thanks.

Carrying the bowl, I stopped before Ivan first. Kalashnik would be last so he had time to appreciate what was coming. My brothers all waited in the shadows.

The blade sliced through his skin like butter as he screamed, "You are all going to die! Fucking biker scum!" Then he let loose a tirade of Russian that I didn't understand, nor care about. When he tried to pull away, he stopped suddenly. Not that he would've been able to get far.

De Luca had simply wanted him ruined. For trying to kill Kira, he wouldn't only be ruined. He'd be dead.

"You must be more stupid than you look in your childish face paint," Kalashnik sneered. Again, I didn't acknowledge him or deign to reply. Anatoly remained stoic and silent. It didn't matter if it was a ruse or if he was truly so brainwashed and cold-blooded that none of this affected him.

Ignoring Ivan's ranting, I continued to carve the appropriate symbols into his chest. The blood that ran from the cuts was collected in the silver bowl.

The only time I interacted with him was when he tried to spit on me. Then I drove the knife up under his chin until the tip pierced the tender flesh behind the bone. Barely above a whisper, I told him, "Spit at me again, and I'll cut out your tongue and slice off your tiny dick, then shove them both down your throat. When I'm done, I'll sew your lips together. You hear me?"

He didn't reply, and I pushed the knife in deeper, making him gasp. He didn't yell, because it would've probably shoved the knife up into his mouth and he knew it. Finally, he replied with little movement of his jaw. "Yes!"

"Good," I replied evenly. Then I finished with him and moved on to Anatoly.

The second the knife pierced his flesh, the beast in me rumbled to life. This was retribution for Kira's childhood he helped destroy. Every cut, every drop of crimson blood, every grunt that it pulled from his blackened soul, fed the beast.

By the time I finished with him, he still remained wordless, but the greenish hue to his face told me I'd affected him. The sweat that was mixing with the blood told me he wasn't completely unfeeling. I'd seriously fought burying my blade in his eye.

Kalashnik had been bitching and threatening the entire time. He really hadn't liked that I'd hurt his baby boy.

Too fucking bad.

When I turned to him, I had to hold myself back. A shiver coursed through me as the demon within shuddered and thrashed. The smell of their blood, the desperate need to end their lives, all of the feelings that went along with it—I knew were part of the me that I despised. My legacy from the demon that called himself my father.

Teeth clenched, I breathed deeply for control. For what he'd done to his own daughter, I wanted to slice his dick into a million pieces. Intently, I stared in his eyes as I allowed my peripheral vision to make the marks I could make in my sleep. Then, I demanded, "Tell me why you were doing business with the Bloody Scorpions."

"Fuck. You," he gritted out. He was soaked with sweat by then, and his skin was clammy. Though I hadn't expected him to answer me, it had been worth a shot. It didn't really matter. Because we'd find out what we needed one way or another.

"You know you're dying, don't you?" I asked in a calculatingly cold voice. My eyes narrowed as I studied him—trying to see what made him tick. With each mark I made, I prayed to get something off him. An image, a flash of his dealings with the Bloody Scorpions—anything.

Except there was nothing.

The longer I spent on their preparation for death the more I wanted to let loose and tear them limb from limb.

Instead, I breathed deep and stilled the angry beast.

Once the marks were made, I chanted low and mixed the dark blood in the bowl with the tip of the knife. The rituals my grandmother had taught me weren't for the weak of heart. Nor were they ones that were openly spoken about. Hell most modern-day practitioners of voodoo and hoodoo didn't know anything about the rituals that were part of my family's legacy.

The tips of my fingers dipped in the still-warm liquid, and I marked each of them as they tried to fight me. It was useless, and all they succeeded in doing was tiring themselves out.

My eyes met Squirrel's, and I knew he'd picked up on what I'd said about Kalashnik knowing he was dying. He would have no reason to answer because he knew he was a dead man walking. His son, however, was his weakness.

"When my men find you, there won't be anywhere for you to hide. You are all dead! You. Your families. Your fucking dogs. Dead!" Ivan was screaming as blood ran down his naked body.

"You're making a bold assumption that anyone has a clue as to where you are." Venom's voice carried out from the shadows.

When I'd made the last mark on Ivan, I stood silent, eyes closed, and prayed. A low murmured chant filled the room on repeat. The candles flickered as I raised my lids from the trancelike state I'd been in.

Just to fuck with them, I shook the chains they were hanging from. Out of the corner of my eye, I saw Phoenix step out of the shadows. The flames on the candles blazed nearly a foot tall before they dropped to their original height. He gave a half smile and faded back.

The fear had finally begun to settle in with the three stooges we had suspended from the ceiling. I could see it in their eyes. I could smell it seeping from their pores. I could hear it in their uneven breaths.

I almost laughed when Ghost appeared from behind me and walked around them slowly with a creepy as fuck tip to his mouth. Not quite a smile, not quite a grimace. He pulled out a wicked-looking blade and stopped behind Anatoly. He gave the dildo a little bounce that caused Anatoly to stiffen slightly. Before anyone knew what was happening, the blade slid through Anatoly's side and retreated.

Anatoly screamed and Kalashnik fought to see exactly what was happening. Ghost slid the knife in the other side to match. Then he disappeared again.

Ivan actually pissed himself. Kalashnik was shouting. Anatoly sagged as his shoulders seemed to pop out of socket.

"Good thing there's a drain," said Raptor with a dark chuckle.

Chains came forward, and I could read the "oh fuck" in Ivan's eyes. He talked a really big game until shit got real. Somehow, I got the feeling he was getting the hint that the cavalry wasn't going to ride in and save them.

The big tatted-up motherfucker cracked his neck, walked up to Kalashnik, and stared at him. Besides the fact that he liked Kira and hated human trafficking, we all owed it to Shank to take a piece of them. First, he punched Kalashnik right in the ribs. The sound of them cracking echoed off the walls.

Walking around behind him, he wrapped his inked fingers around his throat and squeezed. Kalashnik's eyes bugged, and he was gasping for breath. Chains froze, and his eyes met mine over the Russian's shoulder. What I saw there wasn't good, but it wasn't the time to discuss it. He nodded, telling me he'd gotten what we needed.

One by one, each of my brothers took a turn on the three Russians.

By the time everyone was done, they were a bloody, battered mess. Except for their faces. We wanted those to be recognizable. Especially since Anatoly's needed to make a special trip.

Blade, the sick fucker, had peeled the skin off their cocks and shoved it in their mouths. They'd passed out at various times, and we'd used whatever means necessary to revive them.

At the end of it, I took my blade and had it poised to slice Ivan's throat exactly as he'd done to Kira.

"No!"

I froze.

Kira.

TWENTY

Kira

"SCARS"—PAPA ROACH

When Ogun left, I already knew what I was going to do. I'd noticed the folded up clothes on the dresser when he'd brought me in the room earlier. It turned out to be a little harder than I'd anticipated, because I didn't know he'd left a guard dog on me.

Speaking of which, I wanted to pick up my dog in the morning. Knowing she'd been shot and nearly killed had nearly ended me.

Trying not to think about who the items belonged to, I'd gotten dressed and quietly entered the "great hall," as I called it. There was a young guy who was a prospect cleaning the bar and filling the coolers. He'd looked up the second I stepped out of the hall that lead to the rooms.

"Can I get something for you, ma'am?" he'd asked, making me feel old as fuck.

Trying to come up with a reason to be out there, I wandered

to the bar and sat down. "It's so quiet here tonight. Where is everyone? I woke up and it's like a ghost town."

"They had something to do," he said, looking slightly cagey. Kid would need to work on his poker face.

"Hmm. Okay, well, can I get a water?"

"Sure thing," he said with a relieved grin. He pulled one out of the big ice pit behind the bar and set it on one of those paper coasters. The place was really pretty impressive for a private bar.

"I don't suppose you have any snacks, do you?" I asked after I'd already looked around to see if there were any handy. When I didn't see any, I hoped he'd need to go get them from somewhere.

"Umm, well, I was going to restock them, but I haven't gotten that far," he said apologetically.

I pouted in my best fashion.

"I can go get you something if you want," he offered, and I had to fight doing a fist pump.

"That would be awesome." I gave him a bright smile that I prayed looked super innocent but probably looked creepy as hell.

As soon as he went into the kitchen, I hauled ass to the door. "I need to go to the bathroom! Be right back!" I shouted, then quietly went outside. The bikes were still parked alongside the building.

"Where the hell did they go?" I whispered to myself. As I scanned the area, I saw a line of figures at the edge of one of the fields. They were headed onto the neighboring farm. There was enough moonlight that if I was careful, I could probably make my way over there.

It didn't take long to find the path. If I hadn't seen them, I might not have known where to look, but knowing they likely took a fairly straight path, I pushed the lilac bush to the side and there it was.

Praying there weren't any creatures of the night out in the field, I moved cautiously and slow. The night was still, so I could hear their voices carrying across the field but couldn't make out what they were saying.

When I got to the edge of the farm site, I crouched in the plants, because I saw people meandering around the corner of a building set off to the back. My heart was pounding, and it sounded like my breathing was as loud as a chainsaw.

Sometimes at a crawl, I made my way over to a small building surrounded by trees and bushes and leaned against the side like I was in some kind of action movie. "What the hell am I doing?" I asked myself, then slapped a hand over my mouth.

The pigs in the building near me were snuffling around, and I hoped they wouldn't give me away. If I got caught, I knew they'd send me back to the clubhouse and likely lock my ass in the room. I didn't want that, because I really needed to see what they were up to with the three men who'd tried to ruin my life, then kill me.

Peeking around the corner, my eyes bugged as I saw something that sent my insides skittering and my heart froze before pounding against my ribs. The man who'd stepped out of the small building I leaned against looked like a ghoul that would come for your soul. I'd nearly given myself away before I realized it was Ogun.

When he cut through the trees and walked toward the other building, Ghost appeared next to him. I blinked, thinking I'd been seeing things. Then I remembered him doing that when I first woke up. *Holy shit!*

"Voodoo, something's not right," I heard Ghost say. They both paused with the door cracked and simply looked at each other.

"You heard it too?" Ogun whispered, but Ghost shook his head. "Then what?"

"I'm not sure. Lots of whispers that I can't make out. Something has stirred up the spirits. I don't fucking like it." The hogs started to move around more than they had been a minute ago.

"Anyone else sense anything?" Ogun asked his friend before he looked around.

"No."

"Maybe it's just the moon," Ogun murmured. Ghost shrugged. "Stay alert. Let's go in. I'm anxious to get started."

Then they both slipped in the door of the old building. A sigh of relief escaped me until I realized there could be someone out patrolling or whatever they called it. I waited for quite a while and sure enough, a guy came around from the other side.

While I waited, he paced back and forth. Then he walked around the perimeter of the building. He did the same thing a few times, so I figured I'd wait until he turned the corner and haul ass.

Once I determined it was safe to move, I carefully but quickly made my way to the door they'd gone through. Before the guy could come around again, I slipped inside.

There was only one direction I could go, so I followed the hall toward the voices. It was dark and smelled funny in there, but there were lights coming from around the corner at the end of the hall.

At the shouts and groans, I told myself I shouldn't be there—but I needed to be there. The thing was, I didn't know what the hell I was going to do. It wasn't like I had a plan, but I needed to be there. Retribution? Closure? Sick curiosity? Whatever the reason, I needed to be a part of it.

What I watched should've made me ill. It likely should've terrified me. Instead, all I experienced was grim satisfaction. The three of them were getting what they deserved.

Except when I saw the macabre version of the man I'd given my heart to poised to slice Ivan's throat, I couldn't let him do it.

"No!" I shouted. He froze, and his eyes rose to lock on mine. The glint of the red-stained knife in the candlelight was eerie but fascinating. There was a small table with a variety of items spread out on it. Another knife, a pistol, and a good number of things I didn't recognize.

Everyone in the room froze as they warily assessed me. Ghost took a step to the side, and I pointed at him. "I don't know what you were about to do but stop right there."

From the look on his face, he knew I remembered his little disappearing act. Angel was at the other end of the group and calmly watched me with his arms crossed over his chest. Chains stood deep in the shadows, but I saw him as well as the rest of them.

"Is this what you do?" I asked. No one answered me. I ignored the triumphant expression in Anatoly's eyes.

"Answer me! Is this what you do? Torture people and kill them?" I asked in confused outrage.

"Kira," Ogun began, but I silenced him with my hand as I walked around the room, making eye contact with each of them. To their credit, they all boldly met my gaze. Not a one of them flinched. Not to say they didn't have a hint of that wariness still.

Being a veterinarian, I'd learned how to read body language pretty well. Animals only have that to convey what's going on. It wasn't hard to see they all looked poised to pounce on me. Except for Angel. He still calmly watched my movements.

After I'd walked closer to the three men strung up by

chains, I paused by the small table that resembled more of an altar. Before anyone could stop me, I snatched up the pistol. Thankfully, they'd been easy to distract with my act of being horrified. Little did they know, I'd seen worse.

Being raised around the fucking Russian mafia had hardened a part of me, and I'd learned how to use a gun. My brother Viktor had taught me when I was sixteen. After what had happened. So it didn't take me long to ensure a bullet was chambered and point the gun at Ivan.

All of Ogun's brothers moved toward me at once. "Don't," I said, as I held the gun pointed at Ivan. My eyes stayed trained on Ivan, but I watched them all freeze in my periphery.

"Kira. Baby, don't do this. This is something you can't come back from. You can't undo it." Ogun tried his best to convince me, but I was past being swayed.

My chest was heaving, heart racing as the past rushed me like a two-hundred-and-forty-pound defenseman. The three people in front of me had all been party to it. Though Ivan hadn't been there when I was fifteen, he'd threatened to burn off my tattoo, destroy my friends, and he was going to rape me in front of Grishka. Fuck him and his skinned penis.

The first bullet entered right between his eyes. The second in his filleted dick.

"Kira!" Ogun ran at me, and Ghost had his arms wrapped around me in an instant, but not before I'd shot Anatoly in his leg and Grishka in his dick and his stomach. Because I wanted him to suffer.

"Give me the gun, sweetheart," Ghost said in my ear. By then, the adrenaline had started to wear off and I'd begun to shake. Ghost handed me off to Ogun after securing the gun.

Grishka and Anatoly's screams were background noise as he

held me and I buried my face in his neck. The shaking intensified and then the tears started.

"Shh, I've got you." Ogun murmured over and over as he rocked me. Time escaped me as I cried for everything Grishka and Anatoly had been responsible for in my life. The only thing that would've made me happier was if Lester fucking Damen had been there too.

Crying seemed to let loose all the pent-up hurt, frustration, and disbelief of my life.

"That prospect is gonna get his ass handed to him," Venom said from nearby. I felt more than saw Ogun nod. That caused me to look up as I wiped away tears with the back of my hand.

"Please don't. He had no idea. I sent him looking for snacks, then led him to believe I changed my mind and was going back to the room." Worry furrowed my brow.

Ogun's hands framed my face. "It doesn't matter. He knew better than to leave the area unsecured. If you were able to get out without him knowing, someone else could've easily gotten in. It won't be that bad, but he needs to learn."

"But it's not fair that he gets hurt because of me," I argued.

"If he can't handle a little ass-whipping because of a fuckup, he's not cut out to be a Royal Bastard," he replied as he caught a stray tear with his thumb.

A grunt from over my shoulder told me that the others were in agreement. It made me feel bad that he would be punished for something I did, but I also understood it was their club and their rules.

"Voodoo, take her home. We'll finish up here," Venom said from behind us. When I turned to look at him, I could tell he was less than happy with my actions, but I didn't care.

"Let me grab my things. Will you be okay for a minute?" He

clasped my upper arms and leaned down to look me in the eyes. I nodded. His macabre makeup should've been unsettling, but I found it strangely beautiful.

He had the items gathered up quicker than I could've imagined, which told me he'd done this before. What surprised me was that I wasn't bothered by it. Not wanting to analyze why nothing from the night really upset me, I took a deep but shaky breath.

"Come on," he said as he took my hand. We started to walk away, but I stopped and turned to look at Venom.

"I'm not going to say a word. And I hope you kill them both." Then I turned back around and walked with Ogun "Voodoo" Dupré back to the clubhouse.

When we went inside, the prospect seemed shocked to see me coming in the door with Voodoo.

"We'll talk later," Voodoo said to the man, who blanched and swallowed hard.

Once he closed the door to the room, he leaned on it and ran a hand through his hair. "We need to discuss what happened tonight."

"Okay, but I meant what I said. I'm not going to say a word to anyone. I'm not going to fall apart. I'm going to say this explicitly and once. I shot Ivan in the dick because he was going to rape me in front of Grishka; I shot him between the eyes because he had no remorse for trying to kill me—something he would've succeeded in doing had you and your friends not intervened. I shot Anatoly because he's a piece of shit brother who held down his fifteen-year-old sister while she was raped repeatedly for money. My aim was off because I meant to shoot him in the dick too. I shot Grishka in the dick because he doesn't deserve to have it and in the stomach because it wouldn't kill him right away and

I wanted him to suffer for selling me off to the highest bidder not once, but twice, then threatening to sell me and my friend into the sex trade if I didn't comply. I don't regret it, and I'd do it again in a heartbeat." I paused, waiting for his response. The only thing he'd done was cover his own junk when I'd talked about shooting them. It didn't seem like he realized he'd done it, and if the seriousness of the situation wasn't so severe, I might have laughed.

"Regardless, you shouldn't have seen that. It's still your father and your brother. I didn't mean for you to have to see what was going on."

"No. He's not." It was incredible, the relief I experienced at the knowledge that the asshole who'd destroyed my innocence wasn't actually my father.

"What?"

"Grishka isn't my father. He admitted it to me when I was at his house. My father was one of his men. I have no idea if he's alive or dead, but I mean to ask my mother. Yes, Anatoly was my brother, but he was an asshole and a piece of shit. But I need to know something," I said.

"I'll do my best to answer," he warily replied.

"I pieced shit together. Is that what you do? Your club? Are they assassins? Hitmen? Whatever you call it?"

He bit his lip and appeared to weigh the situation and his answer. "Let's just say that we clean house for society. The people that slip through the cracks or get past the system."

Satisfied, I nodded. "Good."

People needed to know that someone was taking out the trash when those who were supposed to, didn't. But it wasn't my place to announce it.

Determined, I walked up to him, grabbed his shirt, and pulled him in for a kiss. Shock held him back for a second. Then, he was all in, his tongue twisting with mine and his teeth tugging on my lip. My fingers sank into his dark hair, and I breathed in the strangely comforting scent that clung to his clothes.

Breaking away gently, he looked at me and grinned. Then his thumb rubbed my lip and chin. "You have my face paint on you."

Pulling him in again, I said against his black-and-white lips, "I don't care. It's kind of sexy."

I got very dirty by the end of it.

TWENTY-ONE

Voodoo

"A WASTED HYMN"—ARCHITECTS

Little did I know that Kira was so perfect for me the first day I'd walked into the vet clinic all those months ago. The club certainly didn't consist of saints, but we liked to think we worked for the greater good. The fact that she didn't freak out when she found out what we were capable of was a relief.

"Baby, we need to shower," I said to her as I looked down at her beautiful body covered in black and white smears. Trying to keep from laughing, I twisted my lips to the side. Cat-like, she stretched in the bed, and I trailed my fingertips along her curves. I'd never met a more beautiful woman inside and out. The fact that she had a little dirty in her was a bonus.

"Mmm, I say we just stay naked and dirty until morning," she murmured sleepily before she rolled to her stomach.

Unable to resist, I leaned over and bit her ass. Not hard enough to hurt, but enough that she certainly felt it. When she purred and raised her ass, I gave her a sharp swat that echoed in the room.

"Hey!" she exclaimed as she rose up to her elbows and looked over her shoulder at me.

"What?" I asked, daring her to tell me she didn't like it.

"Don't tease," she said with a sexy grin. Then she laid her head back down but continued to watch me impishly.

"Hell, woman. You're insatiable," I teased. Her beautifully kiss-swollen lips curled.

Needing to see my brand on her, I pushed her heavy hair to the side. My tongue traced the lines of the ink on her neck. Then I nipped her shoulder and grinned at the goose bumps that broke out across her back and down her arms.

"Get up, or I'm throwing you over my shoulder and bringing you in there my damn self. I want to go home to my bed. It's more comfortable than this one." One last swat, and I stood up. My dick might have been drained, but it still gave a half-hearted thump at the sight of her in my bed.

With a grin, I went into the bathroom.

Getting a look at myself in the mirror had laughter bursting from me. My face paint resembled a melted mime, and there were smeared handprints all over me. "Jesus," I muttered as I soaped up my hands and scrubbed my face. The water ran black for a moment before it was mostly clear.

"Last chance!" I called out as I cranked on the shower.

"I'm here," she said in a seductively husky voice. Again, I tried not to laugh at her. Instead, I gently pulled her into the bathroom to stand in front of the mirror. When she caught a glimpse of herself, she busted a gut laughing.

"Oh sweet Jesus, no wonder you said we needed a shower. I knew we were a mess, but I didn't realize it was that bad." There was almost a perfect impression of my face in black, smeared gray, and white on her stomach. From the look in her eye, she remembered exactly when it had happened too.

We'd already gone one sweaty but quick round. I'd pressed a kiss to her abdomen and rested my tired face against her skin. Things had heated up quickly from there, and our fatigue was forgotten.

"Get in," I rumbled as I swatted her perfect ass again. She now had my handprints on both sides of her ass. It had me wanting to bend her over the sink before we showered, but she'd stepped into the steaming water.

Though it was crowded in the small shower, we managed to get clean. Once we were dried and dressed, we stopped by Venom's room. I had Kira wait off to the side, because one never knew what they might see at one of the brothers' doors.

After I knocked, it was a moment before he answered. Like the rest of the brothers, my president had no shame as he stood there buck-ass naked. Behind him, I saw one of the club whores in his bed. Reya stared me in the eye as she fingered herself, and I quickly averted my gaze. No way was I getting pulled into that shit storm. She was half-crazy, and if Kira caught a glimpse of that hot mess, I'd never hear the end of it.

"We're heading back to my place."

"You sure that's a good idea? We still don't know if Gambler is out there. You know as well as I do that it's likely he is."

"We'll be okay. I'll text you when we get there safe." I waved my phone in the air in front of him before shoving it in my back pocket. As usual, I was packing pretty heavy, so I wasn't too worried.

He didn't look happy, but he nodded. Then he ordered, "You text as soon as you get there."

"Roger that," I replied with a chin lift. "Let's go, babe," I told her as I grabbed her soft hand in mine. I led her out of the clubhouse and to the bikes. The moon was high in the sky, and the crickets were chirping away. Everyone else had either crashed or was buried in wet, willing pussy for the night.

"Can we get Sasha in the morning?" she asked as she buckled the helmet strap.

"If Veronica says she's ready, then yeah."

Rolling her eyes, she huffed. "I'm a vet. Remember? I think I'm qualified to take care of my dog," she replied in a salty tone complete with a smirk.

"Actually, I was more thinking of if it was okay to transport her, not whether you'd be able to handle her." She appeared chagrined as she blinked at me from inside the helmet. Though it was fairly warm, I pulled my leather jacket out of my saddlebag and slipped it over her shoulders. She put her arms in and laughed at how big it was on her.

"Shush. It's better than you getting skinned if something happened. Dress for the slide, not the ride," I said with a slight smile.

"Oh, really? Then why don't you have a helmet on?" was her snarky reply. My answer was another swat to that sexy ass that ended in me clutching it tight in my grip as I pulled her snug against me.

"Don't push me. I will bend this ass over my bike and fuck you compliant right here."

She waggled her brows and grinned. "That seems to be your solution to everything. Threat or a promise?"

A bark of laughter escaped me, I shook my head, and we mounted up.

In the quiet night, we headed down the road. The music was playing on my bike, and my hand rested on her thigh. Wind blew past us and carried all my worries away for the moment.

Though I loved having her on the back of my bike, I wanted to get her back to my bed as quickly as possible. So I took the most direct route that would get us home quicker since traffic was almost nonexistent.

There were very few people on the road at that time of night, so when a single headlight came up quick, I wondered if it was one of the brothers, but put both hands on the grips. "Babe, get my phone out of my pocket," I shouted to her over my shoulder. Something seemed off, and I wasn't taking chances again. "If I say so, you text Venom where we are and what's going on. Okay?"

Her wide eyes met mine in one of my rearview mirrors as she nodded.

The bike came up on us faster than I was comfortable with, so I turned off on a side street. It made the same turn, so I turned back toward the main street. When it made the same turn, I made a signal for her to send the text.

As I sped up and made a few more turns, the bike kept up with us. The second I saw his clutch hand rise and caught the glint of the gun in the streetlight, I yelled to her, "Hold on!"

Taking the corner much faster than I should've, I at least bought us a few minutes, because he needed to use his clutch to downshift on the turn, then accelerate. My heart was racing, and adrenaline was pumping through my veins.

My bike was a bad bitch. Without Kira on the back, I was fairly confidant I could outrun or at least outmaneuver the guy. With her, it complicated things. We zipped up and down the streets—barely staying one step ahead of him.

"Shit!" The truck that pulled out in front of me and slowed down told me I'd inadvertently played right into his hand. With cars parked on both sides of the road, I couldn't make it around them. The bike was closing in fast. We weren't going to make it out of this, and I was sick to my stomach that I'd put Kira in danger.

"When I stop, you get off and haul ass! Take my phone with you! Call Venom!" I yelled back to her.

"No!"

"Goddammit, don't argue with me! I'll hold them off as long as I can!" It was difficult to argue with her and try to operate my bike.

Not waiting for the two fuckers to force my hand, hitting the brakes hard, I stopped on my own. Kira jumped off before I was completely stopped. My heart lurched as she stumbled and fell. She rolled a bit from the momentum, but she got to her knees and ran. The bike behind me nearly hit me, and we both laid our bikes down. I'd have time to worry about the damage later.

Praying she was safe, I grinned when I heard pounding boots behind me. *Dumbasses.* Leading them in the opposite direction, I ran to the other side of the street. Blood pumping and mind racing, I hoped they would continue chasing me. The last thing I wanted to do was pull out my gun and start shooting in a residential neighborhood. No matter how run-down and shitty it was.

Another guy shot out from the shadows in front of me, and I made a quick turn down a side street. Every time I thought I was one step ahead of them, they had cut through a yard or a back street and cut me off. It was okay though, because we were still moving away from where I'd left Kira.

There was an old warehouse not far from where we were. If I could lead them out of the neighborhood, I'd blow a fucking hole in them so big, I could drive my bike through it.

Skating to a stop, I darted through an opening in the fence. Jumping over junk that was scattered around the lot, I headed toward the back. Except as soon as I hooked the corner of the building to pull myself around it, I skidded to a stop.

If I thought my heart was racing before, it had nothing on the out-of-control rhythm that hit me when I was met with a wall of Bloody Scorpions.

Goddamn it. I'd been herded and didn't see it coming.

In fact, that I could've actually handled. Knowing you're going to die isn't the best feeling in the world, but seeing the guy we all knew as Mule with a sick smile was another.

Because he was holding a struggling Kira at the center of their ranks.

To make everything fifty thousand times better, one of their members pushed through to the front to stand next to Mule. My lungs seized. The evil grin on his face was a memory I'd tried to forget.

It was the man I'd thought dead for years.

"My son, you're a hard one to track down," he said as he twirled a piece of Kira's blonde hair around his finger.

Fuck. My. Life.

TWENTY-TWO

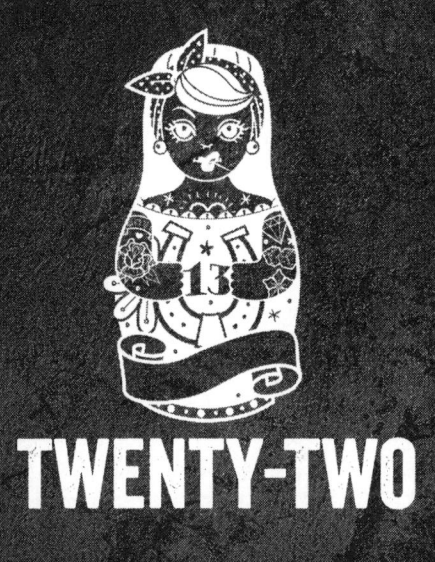

Kira

"LIKE SUICIDE"—SEETHER

I'd done like Ogun had asked, and when I'd dived off the bike, I'd sent a message to Venom. Except I hadn't stopped there, and it wasn't the first message I'd sent. Because when we were on the bike and he first handed me his phone, I sent the message immediately. I'd also sent a group message to everyone in his phone with a local number that was under the RBMC subtitle.

Maybe it was overkill, but I didn't care. Deep in my guts, I'd known things were scarily wrong.

Through every turn and acceleration, I'd held on with one arm, but I'd been keeping them up to date with each move we made. A few times, I almost lost the phone.

After getting my feet underneath me, I'd ripped off the helmet and called Venom. "Where are you?" he'd barked.

"It's me, Kira," I gasped.

Glancing around for a street sign, I saw one up ahead and kept running. Once I was close enough, I let him know and then darted into a backyard where I tried to catch my breath. The connection was horrible, but he'd told me he was on his helmet Bluetooth.

"Please hurry," I panted, and I held the stitch in my side.

"We're en route. Hang up to conserve the battery. Keep that phone on and secured, whatever you do. Facet is tracking you right now. Are you far from Voodoo?"

"I don't know," I whispered breathlessly. "He ran the opposite direction."

"It's okay, we have a general direction. We're on our way. If you're safe there, stay put, and secure that damn phone," he growled, and I swallowed hard as I nodded, though he certainly couldn't see me.

The call ended. I switched the phone to silent so it wouldn't ring or vibrate and waste any of the battery. Then I stashed it in a hidden inner pocket of Voodoo's giant leather jacket and zipped it up. Hoping they would get there soon, I crouched down behind the trash cans I'd stopped by.

Everything was silent, but I thought I heard the roar of motorcycles in the distance. Moving cautiously, I stood enough to look over the trash cans. Slowly, I moved in a crouch up along the dark shadows of the house so I could see if it was them.

I'd almost reached the front of the house where I could hide in the bushes when a pebble skidded along behind me and made me freeze. Heart in my throat, I spun around.

"Well, hello, gorgeous. We meet again. Except this time, I don't have to hand you off to anyone but my brothers. Fucking Russians fuck up everything." The younger of the two men who'd taken me to Chicago stood there with a gun trained on my chest. The side of his face with the scorpion tattoo was in the shadows of the streetlight, but I'd know that voice anywhere.

"Turn around real slow-like and put those hands behind your head," he drawled as he moved closer to me. Shaking and wanting to cry in frustration, I simmered as he cable-tied my hands behind my back.

Where the fuck were the people who lived in the neighborhood? Didn't anyone hear anything? It shouldn't surprise me though. People in that area of town probably didn't stick their noses into anything that happened after the sun went down.

"Move," he snarled as he shoved me forward. It caused me to trip, and I thought I was going down on my face because I couldn't use my hands. I'd like to say I was thankful that he grabbed me by the cable tie and jerked me upright, but truthfully, it hurt like a bitch. It seemed like my shoulders popped out of socket, but I barely made a peep. I wouldn't give him the satisfaction.

We didn't walk long, because as we neared the street corner, the same shitty truck I'd ridden to Chicago in stopped. At least they didn't shove me in the back again, but I was shoved face-first into the back seat. They went around a few corners but we didn't travel far.

The rattle of a chain-link gate was followed by it closing behind us. They didn't go far before they parked the truck and killed the engine. The door was flung open, and the asshole dragged me out my by ankles, then my wrists, causing my shoulders to scream in agony again.

"Easy, you asshole! My arms are about to pop out of socket!" I was fed the fuck up with being abducted and beat around. Twice in less than a week was really too damn much. I was pissed.

"You think I care? I don't need your arms to fuck that hole of yours," Scorpion-face jeered, and I wanted to head-butt him. He grabbed a cut out of the truck and gave me a shove.

Taking in my surroundings, I realized we were in an old warehouse or retail store parking lot. There was a fence around it intended to deter people, but these yahoos obviously didn't care about shit like private property.

"Well, what do we have here?" One of the club members saw us approach, and as we neared, they all turned around. They didn't look much like Ogun's club. Most of them looked motley and unkempt. There was one guy who was extremely good-looking, but he stayed to the back, looking unhappy. All in all, there was about six or seven of them.

Then again, they all looked miserable.

The voice that had called out separated from the crowd, and I groaned.

"What, you aren't happy to see me? Looks like dear ol' dad wasn't able to keep you long. Not my problem. I got paid to get you there, not keep you there," the older guy said with a smirk. I didn't dignify him with a response. When they'd grabbed me outside the vet clinic, I hadn't gotten much of a chance to get a good look at him.

He'd obviously been decent-looking once. As he came closer, I could tell that time hadn't been kind to him, and if his blown pupils were any indication, he was high as a kite. The name on his cut read "Gambler."

"That her?" asked a big burly guy with a beard and an eye patch.

"Yep, that's her," Gambler said with a grin that showed dirty teeth. That's when I realized there was a scar that intersected his top and bottom lips and went up to near his eye. Any closer, and he might've lost it.

"Good. Now we wait," one of the other guys said from the group.

"I can't believe you two idiots didn't catch him after he laid down the bike," another guy said with a disgusted shake of his head.

"That motherfucker is fast as fuck," grumbled Scorpion-face.

"Well, he obviously didn't get it from you, Gambler," the burly guy said with a laugh.

"Fuck off," muttered Gambler. My mind was reeling when what the guy said settled into my brain. Was the other guy implying that this was Ogun's father? If I had to guess, he was easily in his sixties, but then again, he might've just had a hard life.

The resemblance was definitely there. The eyes mostly. Maybe the height. Ogun's coloring had to have come from his mother's side.

Scorpion-face had his cut on now, and it read "Skid." It made me wonder if the asshole didn't know how to wipe his ass. It almost made me laugh. And I still preferred Scorpion-face.

"They're coming!" said a guy from over in the shadows of the lot.

A squeal of surprise escaped me when one of them grabbed the back of my hair and held it tight.

My heart soared and fell when Ogun came racing around the building. When he saw me, his face fell, and I swear I wanted to cry. It seemed like we simply couldn't win.

Gambler pushed through the crowd to stand next to me.

"My son, you're a hard one to track down," Gambler said next to me as he played with a piece of my hair. "Over twenty-five years I've looked for you. Then again, for a few of those I was recuperating and rehabilitating from being tortured and beaten, then dumped in the fucking swamps. All thanks to your grandfather and those fucking Pussy Bastards."

"Tie him up," the one with the eye patch said to his flunkies.

Panic bubbled up in me at what they might do to him when he couldn't defend himself. Not that the odds were great even if he wasn't restrained.

The rage flickered in his eyes like flames. The debris that littered the lot began to move as if a strong wind had picked up, but there was nothing. My hair was still except for the light breeze that had been there before.

Startled, the bad guys, as I decided to call them, began to look around nervously. When several of the old windows shattered and the glass impaled a couple of them, they really got nervous.

"What the fuck?" one of them shouted.

The only one who wasn't panicking was the man I believed to be Ogun's father. When I glanced his way, he was staring at Ogun with a narrowed gaze.

"It would seem you learned a few new tricks over the years," murmured Gambler. "Either you stop, or I kill her. Because I really don't need her. It's you and those magic tricks of yours I'm after."

The cold steel against my head made me freeze, barely breathing. All of the trash and debris dropped to the ground. There were murmurs of disbelief around me from the other club. Ogun stood there, chest heaving.

"If I go with you and don't give you any trouble, you let her go," he bargained.

"No!" I reflexively cried out. In my heart, I hoped Venom and the rest would get there soon. I could've sworn I'd heard bikes before. *Where are they?*

"Kira, please. I'll be okay."

"Yeah, Kira. He'll be okay," Gambler said in a sarcastic, condescending manner.

"Hurry up and get over here," said the one with the eye patch whose cut said Mule. It was apparent that Ogun didn't want to give in, but he was willing to sacrifice himself for me. I hated it.

"Let her go," Ogun demanded when he was halfway to them.

"You think we're stupid? Hell, no. Not until your ass is secured." I think it was Scorpion-face that said that, but I couldn't be sure.

His jaw clenched and his eyes flashed, but he continued forward. With each step, I bit my lip harder until I tasted the coppery tang of blood. Each breath was painful and each heartbeat agony, as I knew he was walking closer to our end.

Finally, he stood close enough I could smell a faint hint of his shower gel and the exhaust from the bike. More than anything, I wanted to reach out and touch him. Feel his arms wrapped around me. Hear him tell me he was going to get us out of this. Taste his lips on mine.

"Turn around," Gambler ordered. Ogun's nostrils flared, and I could hear his teeth grind in tightly leashed anger. Still, he did what he was told, and I flinched as I heard the cable ties tighten. The gun dropped from my head, and I breathed a partial sigh of relief.

As soon as they were tight, Ogun turned to face them. "Now let. Her. Go," he said with bared teeth.

Several of them laughed. My eyes darted around as Ogun's jaw worked and his body tensed.

"Now why would we do that?" Mule asked. "If we let her go, how will we keep you in line? Something tells me you'll be a bit more amenable to our needs if me or one of my brothers has a cock about to go up her pretty little ass." He laughed, as did the majority of the group.

"You dirty motherfuckers!" he roared as he lunged at the

nearest guy. It didn't seem to matter to him that his hands were fastened behind his back. Mule didn't hesitate for a second. He raised his hand and shot Ogun, who spun and fell to the ground as I screamed.

"Shut her up!" Mule growled. Skid slapped me across the face so hard I saw stars, stunning me into silence.

"What the fuck did you do that for?" Gambler yelled at Mule. Then he told another guy to get Ogun in the truck.

Right as they were dragging Ogun toward the truck I'd been in, there was a quiet *pop*. The guy dragging him stopped, blood trailing from a hole in his head, and he dropped like a rag doll. The sound he made as he hit the cracked asphalt was one I'd likely never forget.

The guy I'd noticed as out of character with the Bloody Scorpions pulled a gun and searched the area wildly. His nostrils flared as he swallowed hard and glanced in an oddly longing way at the guy with the blood pooling under his head. When he looked back up, our eyes locked and I noticed a shimmer in his that seemed almost animal-like. Without batting an eye, he shot one of his own guys who had started shooting wildly around them.

"What the fuck?" Mule shouted before he too was missing the back of his head and lying lifeless at my feet.

Gambler grabbed my hair and pulled me in front of his body. He was using me as a human shield. My mouth fell open as another one of the guys dropped to the ground. Blood spurted from his neck wound. He tried to hold it for mere seconds before it was apparent he was gone.

Out of the corner of my eye, I saw Skid scaling the fence, but I was terrified to scream, because Gambler held his damn gun to my head.

"Gambler. Let her go. It's not worth it," the guy tried to reason with him. I had no idea what his name was because his cut only said "prospect."

"Shut up, prospect! You killed one of our patches!" he screamed in my ear. The prospect guy tried to reason with Gambler.

"He was going to bring the cops in. He was shooting erratically. Not to mention, innocent people could've been harmed as well. Chill out, Gambler. Let her go and let's get out of here. She's only going to slow us down." His eyes held mine again, and I knew he was trying to get me to understand something. The problem was, I had no idea what.

When he kept looking at me then down, I took a calculated risk, made myself dead weight, and dropped. My knees hit the hard asphalt, and I whimpered. He shot Gambler, causing him to stumble back from me. Because I had no way to catch myself, I fell forward and whacked my chin on the ground.

Groaning, I rolled to my side.

The prospect seemed to be the only one of the Bloody Scorpions still standing. He carefully sat me up. As he assessed me for damage, his hands framed my face. Then, his eyes shimmered again, and he leaned in. In shock, I sat there as his lips brushed mine and his tongue ran along my bleeding lip.

Except, he definitely wasn't kissing me. Because he then held his tongue under my chin where warm blood was continuing to drip.

"If you don't get your mouth off my woman's face, I'll peel your skin from your body." It was said in a pained and growling tone, and I sucked in a startled breath as I saw Ogun struggling to sit up.

The prospect pulled out a wicked-looking blade, and I

paused. There wasn't any need to be concerned, though. He only sliced the ties from around my wrists before moving over to do the same for Ogun.

Except he hesitated. Then he said, "If I cut you loose, you can't kill me."

Through gritted teeth, Ogun said, "You're not in a position to barter. In case you didn't notice, your club members are dead."

"They weren't my club and they certainly aren't my people," the man spat in disgust as he cut Ogun free anyway. He even helped him sit up as Ogun groaned and winced in pain. When he brought the knife toward Ogun's neck, I cried out.

"Please don't!" The man raised a brow at my outburst, gave me a half smile, and sliced through Ogun's T-shirt. He did it again and pulled the pieces off to wad up and press to the wound on Ogun's shoulder. Ogun flinched and nodded.

"Thank you. I owe you." Ogun held the man's gaze, but I didn't like his labored breathing, and I still wasn't sure who had been doing the shooting. Nor did I know where they were. It was like they were ghosts.

"Lay back," he said to Ogun, who reluctantly obeyed. Gambler groaned behind me, and I whipped my head his direction. He wasn't going anywhere, but I still scooted away from him.

"Kira," Ogun gasped out. I crawled over to him. "There's a gun in the pocket of that jacket. Get it out."

Fumbling, I checked the pockets and found a small pistol. He nodded at me. I chambered a round and held the weapon pointed at Gambler. Brow furrowed, I glanced around. "I think Skid got away."

"Who the fuck is Skid?" Ogun grunted.

"A Bloody Scorpions member. Piece of shit," the guy muttered.

"Why are you helping me?" Ogun asked as he stared up at the man who was holding pressure on his wound.

"Because I hate them. I was only with them because I've been looking for a young girl who went missing. Everything I found pointed to them, so I was trying to get close to them to see what I could find out." The guy's breathing became labored, and he seemed pale to the point that he looked green.

"Are you okay?" I asked him as worry furrowed my brow. "You really don't look too good."

He swallowed with difficulty. "It's all this blood," he rasped. I took over with the compress as the guy fell back to his ass. We both looked up as we heard motorcycles closing in on us.

A guy all in black was racing down the road toward us, carrying what looked like a musical instrument case. *What the fuck is going on?*

Blinking in disbelief, I watched as familiar figures skidded to a stop near us and jumped off their bikes. They were much more graceful at it than I had been.

Angel ran toward us and gently removed my hands. "I've got it, babe," he said softly, and a tear slipped from my eye. I clasped Ogun's hand in mine as I sniffled. Then I realized Phoenix was pointing his gun at the man who'd helped us, and I scrambled to get his attention.

"Wait! Phoenix! He helped us! He's a friend!" I spouted.

Phoenix's lip curled. "His cut says otherwise."

The guy was shaking his head, and if it was possible, he looked worse. Imagine my shock when he crawled over to Mule and bit him.

No shit, he literally leaned over and bit his goddamn neck. He wasn't there long before he sat back up but dropped his head. His back heaved as he breathed heavily. When he slowly raised his head and turn our direction, I gasped. There was blood all over his lips, and for a second I would've sworn I saw fucking fangs.

"Uh, dude. You okay?" Squirrel asked with his eyes wide.

"I think he's a fucking vampire," Ghost murmured.

"What? Hell, no. There's no such thing," Squirrel argued.

Chains chortled. "Listen to you, you dumb fuck. If you asked the average person out there, they wouldn't believe the shit we can do."

"Enough," Venom said. Then he turned to the guy in black. "Thanks, Reaper. You have no idea how glad I was to hear you were in town. I can't thank you enough for helping out."

The guy in black shrugged and shook Venom's hand. "Anytime. Hell, I was literally right down the road picking up a bike. You're lucky I travel with my baby." He raised the instrument case that obviously didn't hold an instrument. Well, not a musical one, anyway.

Through everything, my eyes were bouncing from person to person, and my bleeding chin was damn near dragging the ground. It was like I was stuck in the middle of a crazy dream.

"Close your mouth before you catch flies."

My head swiveled to Ogun. My hand squeezed his, and I burst into tears. It was too much. Everything that had happened in such a short time was completely surreal.

"Shh," he said as he sat up with Angel's help. Angel looked like he'd pulled an all-nighter. Where I'd been holding the wadded-up fabric was a slightly scarred spot. My hand unconsciously went to my neck where I had a thin line much like the small circle on Ogun's shoulder.

"I think I need a drink," I whispered.

TWENTY-THREE

Voodoo

"WHAT I LIVE FOR"—ROB BAILEY & THE HUSTLE STANDARD

"Jesus fucking Christ, I'll be glad when shit settles down around here," grumbled Chains as he took a long pull from his bottle.

"You and me both." I sighed as I did the same. Kira wiggled in my lap, and I swatted her ass playfully. "Sit still."

Drunk as a skunk, she giggled. There was no way I was getting pussy that night, and I didn't need her teasing me like that. If she kept it up, I was heading to bed with blue balls. Big fucking blue balls.

"I think I need another drink!" she cheerfully announced. "How about you, Calix?"

The vamp sitting at the table with us made me a little uneasy. Not that he'd done anything wrong to us. In fact, I likely owed him more than I could ever repay. That's why our club was about to do him a solid, and if he took us up on the offer, great—if not, so be it.

"I'm good, thanks," he said with a wry tip of his lips. I had yet to see fangs, so I wondered how that shit worked. Did he ever cut his own tongue or lips? A guy has questions about shit like that.

"Hey, baby, why don't you go up to the bar and have the prospect make you a Raging Gorilla? I think it'll be just what you need." The rest of the brothers tried to hide their grins and laughter. She was oblivious, thank fuck.

"Is it good?" she asked with one squinted eye, her lips twisted to the side and one brow raised.

"You'll love it," I solemnly promised.

She smiled wide, stood up, and wobbled. My hands grabbed her hips to hold her steady. I gave her a questioning look, and she waved her hands at me. "I'm perferlectly fine," she slurred a little as she stumbled over her words. She leaned toward Calix and actually touched his lip with her index finger. "You gotta show me those things before you go."

"Sorry, man," I apologized, but he smiled and gave a good-natured shrug.

"It's no problem."

Once I knew she could walk without falling over, I let her go.

"Bro, that's fucked-up. You know that's a nonalcoholic drink, right?" Angel asked with a smirk as he sipped his whiskey neat.

"Duh," I said incredulously. "Did she look like she needs more?"

"Aww, give her a break. She's had her mind blown over the past week." Phoenix chuckled as he played with a lighter. He bounced the flame from the lighter, then along his fingertips and back to the lighter. Our new friend stared in awe.

I chuckled. "You have mystical teeth and drink blood, but you're amazed by his magic tricks?"

Calix laughed. "I guess so."

"Fuck off. It's not magic tricks," muttered Phoenix. Then he sent the flame over to the top of my drink, where it flared before I blew it out.

"Asshole."

Everyone laughed.

Venom raised his drink and studied our new friend for a minute before he spoke. "Look, Calix. I'm not sure if you have, um, people here, or what your plans are, but I had an idea."

Sweet Jesus. Please don't let him have people around here.

He sighed heavily and ran a hand over his face before dropping it to the tabletop. "No. No people. They're all up in Alaska. I'd rather not discuss my circumstances, but I'm definitely here alone."

Thank fuck for small favors.

Venom continued. "Well, then this might work out well for you. It might be something that would interest you, since you said you only... uh... dine... on shitbags." We'd had a pretty extensive conversation on the way back to the clubhouse about why he'd hooked up with the Bloody Scorpions.

Venom, Raptor, and I were the only ones who knew about the Tennessee chapter's members because they kept things extremely quiet. The only reason we knew at all was because of one of my visions.

He drew in a deep breath. "So we have this chapter in Rock Bottom, Tennessee. They do some crazy shit to help kids that are in bad situations. They're your kind of people."

It was by far one of the most bizarre conversations I'd ever witnessed. That's saying a lot, because I lived and worked with guys that could do some pretty amazing shit.

He raised a dark brow and gave me a sardonic smirk. "My kind of people as in vampires?"

"Dude. I didn't mean anything by it," I offered. He slouched back in his chair and dropped his head.

"I understand. Sorry, I'm not exactly used to people welcoming me with open arms when they find out what the fuck I am. Trust me, I didn't ask for this life. Anyway, so you think they'd want dick shit to do with me if they find out I was a prospect for those assholes?" His head lifted and his eyes held mine.

"Only one way to find out. We can give them a call tomorrow. In the meantime, I have a drunk-ass woman to put to bed and business to tend to before *I* can go to bed." My gaze found Kira where she was leaning on the bar, talking animatedly with Raptor. Finishing my drink, I shoved away from the table.

"I'll show you where you'll be sleeping," offered Angel. "Wait. You guys do sleep, right?"

Calix laughed. "Yeah, man. We sleep."

Angel raised his glass to Calix. "Cool. Cheers." Calix raised his drink, and they both finished. I stood to collect my woman.

"I'll meet you all back out here as soon as I get her settled." Phoenix and Chains nodded.

"We can wait until tomorrow night if you want." Venom offered as he stopped at the table.

A chill shot through me. "No. The sooner the better."

Venom nodded and pulled up a seat at the table. He was talking quietly with Calix as I wove through the scattered tables to get to Kira.

My hands slid around her and palmed her flat stomach. Pulling her snug to my front, I kissed the side of her neck.

"Mmm, hey, sexy. I was just enjoying that drink you said I'd like." Her eyes got comically wide as she looked over her shoulder at me. "It's sooooo good," she groaned. My lips quirked.

"Well, by all means, finish it up and then let's go to bed."

She gave me a deeply satisfied look, and I laughed. "Sleep."

Pouting, she turned in my arms and looked up at me. "We were supposed to be at your house tonight. In your giant bed. The least you could do is give me a little something to make up for us having to crash in the dinky bed."

"It's a queen size. It's not dinky." I smirked. Granted, it wasn't as big as my bed at home, but it was far from tiny.

"You're a big guy. You make it a small bed." That was her drunken argument. I took her hand and led her back toward my room.

"Goodnight, everyone!" she called out with a big wave. "I'm gonna get him naked and take advantage of me. Um, wait. I mean I'm gonna take advantage of him." Her confused expression was cute as fuck.

"Come on, drunk-ass. Move." I swatted her ass and she then led me.

I needn't have worried, because I'd no sooner gotten her in the room and undressed before she was zonked in the bed softly snoring. Maneuvering the blankets out from under her, I covered her up and kissed her head.

"I love you, Kira Baranov."

She didn't answer, but a sweet, soft smile curled her lips.

We'd been working dear ol' Gambler over for about an hour. He'd admitted that he'd convinced his Louisiana chapter to allow him to make the jump up to South Des Moines when he got an anonymous tip that I was alive and well in the middle of Iowa. They had hoped to use my ability of precognition to their advantage. As if it worked that way.

Turned out, Grishka Kalashnik had hired them to do his dirty work with Kira. They'd been watching her and that was how they'd found me, but they didn't want to mess with me here on my turf. They thought if they helped him get her up to Chicago, it would send me chasing after her—which it had. Then they were planning to grab me up there. Dumb shits hadn't counted on my brothers going with me.

"How's it feel, *Dad?*" I snidely asked as I held the cold steel of my pistol to his temple. "You think this is how Mom felt?"

"I doubt it. Because unlike your worthless mother, I don't care." He spat blood out onto the heavy-duty plastic under him.

"That's a shame," I crooned in his ear. "Because this isn't how you're going to go out. Maybe you'll care after Squirrel has a little fun with you. See, I'm not the creative one. I'm just very good at cleaning up messes." I'd already left the marks on him to trap his soul from reincarnation. Plus, I'd had my bit of fun with him strapped to the chair. My work was essentially done.

"Can you handle this piece of shit?" I asked Squirrel and Blade, who both solemnly nodded. Rael leaned against the wall. His face was painted black and white, much like mine was, and I saw the glimmer of his reaper in his eyes. It sent a shiver skating down my spine, yet I still grinned evilly. "Good, because I have my ol' lady to get back to." Then I returned my attention to my sperm donor. "You have fun now, okay?"

Rael walked with me out the door. "You sure you needed me? It seemed like you had shit under control."

He was referring to my ability to "kill" Gambler's soul.

"No. Because I wanted him to suffer for as long as possible, and I want it to be excruciating. Because of him, my ol' lady nearly died, and my mother was forced to leave the only home she ever knew and endured more abuse than any one person should ever have to endure. I appreciate you and Patriot flying all the way out here to do this for me on such short notice."

He gave me a wicked grin. "We don't mind one bit. Hell, you're the one who paid for the astronomically expensive last-minute flight. I'm just happy for you, brother. Having an ol' lady is a wild ride." He shook his head with a half-smile.

"So I hear."

We shook hands, and I slowly made my way back to the clubhouse. Thoughts filled my head as I placed one foot in front of the other. After feeding him a story about Kira's abduction, I'd arranged with Dr. Moran to get her a few more days off work. I'd planned to pick up Zaka and Sasha and take her to look for a new place to live.

After all, my duplex would never accommodate Me, Kira, Zaka, Sasha, and the changes I had seen coming in my vision.

Despite all the shit of the past couple of hours, I grinned.

EPILOGUE

Voodoo

Five months later...

My hand slid over the baby bump that Kira carried with her typical sexy aplomb. It was hot as Hades, yet she still managed to look beautiful. Hair twisted up in a bun, she pulled off pregnant elegance like no one's business.

She'd also stayed active, busy, and refused to let me coddle her, much to my disappointment. She was carrying my baby, and I worried about her. It was my right, in my opinion. The one thing she did do for me was stop working so many hours. She no longer worked Saturdays at the clinic, and they'd hired another vet to help out.

"What's up with Angel?" she asked as she glanced in his direction. He was pacing as he spoke on the phone and making wild gestures.

"I only know a little of it, and it's not my story to tell. He'll be okay." I hoped I was right.

"I hope so." Kira's words mirrored my own worry. She chewed on her lip as she watched Angel pull at his hair. Then she sighed, turned to me, and looped her hands around the back of my neck. Her hard belly pressed against me, preventing her from getting too close. "Are you ready to head to the airport?"

"Only if my fiancée will give me a kiss first." Those beautiful lips of hers curled, and her hazel eyes twinkled before she stood on her toes and kissed me.

She tasted divine, and I was one second away from carrying her off to my room in the clubhouse to ravage her pregnant body. Because pregnant sex was the fucking bomb. No, we hadn't been planning a baby, but with all the shit that went down with her father, then my father, she'd missed a few pills.

Ask me if I cared.

"We have to go," she said against my lips as she broke the kiss.

"I thought you two had to get to the airport?" Chains asked as he walked in the door behind us. "Now, if you want to put on a show for me, I'm all about watching."

Kira's face flamed as he chuckled under his breath. Between the three of us, we all knew it was a secret little reminder that Kira had been transfixed by him getting sucked off all those months ago. That had led to hot monkey sex in my room and the beginning of the end, so to speak.

A door opened, and nails clicked on the concrete floor before Zaka and Sasha burst out of the back hall. A frazzled prospect came running after them. "I'm so sorry! I think they sensed that you hadn't left yet, because they opened the damn door!"

We both laughed as we gave them love. "I'll help him," said Venom as he clasped both dogs' collars. "But get out of here before you miss your plane."

After saying our goodbyes again, we headed down the road.

"By this time tomorrow we'll be in New Orleans!" Kira said with excitement. She'd been over the moon when my grandmother insisted we visit.

"You know my grandmother is going to insist we stay with her, right?" I asked as I took a second to glance in her direction.

"Are there alligators out there?" she asked with wide eyes and a furrowed brow.

"Maybe a few, but I'd wrestle all of them for you." It was corny as hell, but it made her laugh, and that's all that mattered.

The rest of the trip to the airport was filled with her chatter that kept a smile on my face. The flight was more of the same. By the time we'd switched planes and finally landed at Louis Armstrong, she was almost jumping up and down.

She was like a kid, and I doubted I'd smiled more at any point in my life. Her childlike enthusiasm was adorable.

As soon as we stepped out of the security area, my grandmother was standing there waiting with open arms. I hugged her tightly. "Granmé," I murmured fondly before I broke away to make introductions.

"Kira, this is my grandmother, Adelaide Laveaux. Granmé, this is Kira."

Her pale blue eyes took Kira in from head to toe as she held Kira's hands, and a soft smile tipped her lips. "She will bear you strong sons and a lovely daughter. You've chosen well."

Rolling my eyes a little at my grandmother's teasing, I fought the laughter that threatened to erupt at Kira's saucer-like eyes.

"We decided not to find out the sex of the baby," she whispered in awe. My grandmother laughed and scoffed.

"Madame Laveaux needs no ultrasound," she said with a

dismissive wave of her hand before she chuckled. She hooked her arm through Kira's and began to lead her off toward baggage claim. The look Kira shot over her shoulder at me when my grandmother started talking about what she believed the baby's abilities would be was hilarious.

Once we gathered our bags, the three of us made our way out to the car. A huge grin broke out when I saw who was leaning against it with his arms folded.

Jameson pushed off from the vehicle and met me halfway. We embraced, and I made my introductions. "What the fuck are you doing here?"

"Couldn't let Madame Laveaux drive herself. The entirety of New Orleans would be in danger." He raised a brow as my grandmother stood with arms akimbo, glaring.

"Don't make me put a hex on you, *beau diable*! I'll make it so your wee willy refuses to stand upright for a month." Jameson's hands both covered his junk as he gave her a disbelieving, concerned stare.

"Now, no need to get drastic here," he argued darkly, as we all laughed and he glared at me. "Jesus, Voodoo! Do something."

"You're on your own with this one, brother!" I chuckled. "She already blessed me with a passel of boys and a girl!"

"God help us all," he muttered as he shook his head.

What I didn't tell Kira, because I doubted she was ready to hear it, was that my grandmother's predictions for children were uncannily accurate. In fact, people came from miles away to seek her out for exactly that.

Laughing, we all got in the car and headed to a part of New Orleans few people who visited actually got to see.

Back in the swamps, deep in the bayou off the east side of the river, there was a quiet cabin.

You had to know where you were going to get there, and you could only get there by boat. Dark as pitch when the sun went down. Frogs, creatures of the night, and the beasts that dwelled under the murky water were your travel companions.

If one was lucky enough to be welcomed, you'd knock twice. No more, no less, and wait. Those were Granmé's rules.

Jameson quietly guided the boat through the swamp. Kira held my hand tightly the entire way.

"Come inside, children. I must read her cards," my grandmother instructed when the boat hit the dock. We followed her in after I promised Jameson we'd swing by the clubhouse to see everyone the next day.

"This is amazing," Kira whispered to me as we trailed behind my crazy grandmother with a flair for the dramatic.

Through a doorway at the back of the house, behind red and black beads, was her sanctuary. She welcomed us in, and we took a seat at the other side of her table.

While voodoo was a very serious belief system, this was fairly new to Kira. I'd only briefly shown her my sanctuary in my basement. She'd been fascinated, but skeptical.

My grandmother lit candles, then mixed herbs and roots in a dish before lighting it as well. Then she picked up her tarot deck. The delicate silver knife went in her right hand, and the silver rings on her fingers glinted in the candlelight.

She'd taught me as a young boy that silver restored stability in a person's spiritual energy and protected from the dark energy that tried to get in. I'd taken every lesson to heart.

Finally, she cut the deck and motioned for Kira to touch the cards. Slowly, she revealed each card, one by one, studying them as she laid them down. It was the same process every time. One that I'd been taught and cultivated.

As she studied them together, she absently whirled the small knife through her fingers.

She prayed over the cards, and I knew Kira was experiencing the peace that washed over us as she completed her ritual. Then she spoke.

"You have been through much, but there is someone new in your life. Not Ogun. Someone new but old." My grandmother frowned. "A father that is not a father, and one that is but couldn't be." Though my grandmother seemed slightly confused, Kira gasped. We both knew what my grandmother didn't about Grishka and Aleksandr.

"The one that couldn't was thought to be dead, but he isn't. You must find him, because he's the father of all." She appeared confused, but Kira sobbed. She hadn't mentioned to her mother what Grishka had told her, because we assumed Aleksandr had been killed.

It almost sounded like her other brothers may belong to Aleksander as well.

"But how? If Grishka knew immediately that you weren't his, how did he not know your brothers weren't his? And how did Alexsandr still have access to your mother?"

"Viktor and Dmitry look like my mother. I always assumed I looked like someone else from the family. Maybe Grishka lied or only assumed my brothers were all his." Kira appeared thoughtful.

After the reading, Kira called her mother, who was tearful when she found that the man she'd had a passionate affair with might still be alive. I promised to help her find answers and sent a text off to Facet with the information I had.

We enjoyed every day that we spent in my old home.

Kira had been welcomed into the family by the brothers and

the families of the New Orleans chapter. She couldn't believe that all the way across the country, I was as loved and accepted as in my home chapter.

Before we knew it, it was time to head home.

My grandmother cradled Kira's cheeks in her beringed fingers as we stood outside of the security checkpoint saying our goodbyes. "You take good care of my Ogun. He's a good boy, and you'll never find a soul more loyal, for the love between you two is strong."

Then she turned to me with a soft smile. "Godspeed and safe travels."

One last lingering hug and promises to visit again after the baby was born were exchanged. My grandmother was tearful but trying to act tough.

"Go on! Get, before you miss your airplane." She made a shooing motion, and I kissed her wrinkled cheek.

Right as we were getting ready to pass through the gate, she called out to me. "Remember what I told you? Love always wins, Ogun."

I grinned as I wrapped an arm around my beautiful woman. Hell, yeah, it did.

The End

ACKNOWLEDGEMENTS

How fitting is it that my thirteenth full-length published book is titled Voodoo? It must've been destiny. I hope you all enjoyed him and are ready for his brother, Angel. Yes, this series has been a tiny bit darker than my norm and I hope you can forgive me for that.

This part usually gets a little out of hand. So I'm thanking you all.

With a special shout out to my family who has hung in there as I religiously pounded out this story. Wow, that sounded dirty. Eh, go figure.

Thank you to the authors who have been part of the Royal Bastards MC group. This has been an experience I will never forget. It has cultivated friendships I will treasure forever, made me laugh, made me cry, and been all around badass. Especially to **Crimson Cruz** and **Nikki Landis** for organizing it and **Kristin Youngblood** for keeping us in line. Y'all are my idols.

Thank you **Kristin** for being my Beta reader, too. You kept me motivated and ensured I was on the right track with this one. Not to mention, you've been a lifesaver of a PA! Love you bunches, babe!

Thank you to my street team, but especially **Wynter Raven**, **Stracey Ishwar**, and **Pam Schultz** who always go above and beyond! Y'all have been amazing.

Penny. Where do I even begin? My friend, co-worker, soon-to-be nurse, I love you bunches! I said this same thing before, but you're actually starting the nursing program now and I'm so proud of you. You and you alone, are responsible for the courage

I found to publish Colton's Salvation in May 2017. You were beside me the entire way. You shared in the heartache of rejection, the perseverance to self-publish, and the elation when that first book became a success beyond my wildest dreams. So thank you for always believing in me. Even when I didn't believe in myself. <3

Lisa and Brenda, my two book-loving friends, turned part-time PA's. What would I do without the advice, support and encouragement from you both? You've been lifesavers. Your knowledge of the book world and signing events have been a Godsend. I'm bummed that the stupid COVID ruined our book signing plans for this year, but next year is gonna be wild.

Jay Aheer, Thank you for putting up with me through this cover design process. I promise I wasn't trying to be a diva. LOL.

Eric McKinney, thank you for your incredible image of **Gus Smyrnios**. Eric, you are a photographic genius and a sweetheart. **Gus**, thank you for gracing my cover!

Stacey, as usual, you're a goddess. You always make the inside of my books look beautiful, professional, and badass! I could never convey the amount of thankfulness I feel for you. You're the best!

Ladies of **Kristine's Crazy Fangirls**, y'all are the motherfreaking bomb! I thank you for your comments, your support, and your love of books. Come join us if you're not part of the group!

As I often do, I found a way to spin the military into the storyline. I feel drawn and compelled to do this often because the military has had such a huge impact on my life. From being a military brat, to a military spouse, and working as a nurse in the military system. With that being said, my last-but-never-least, is a massive thank you to America's servicemen and women who protect our freedom on a daily basis. They do their duty, leaving their families for weeks, months, and years at a time, without asking for praise or thanks. I would also like to remind the readers that not all combat injuries are visible nor do they heal easily. These silent, wicked injuries wreak havoc on their minds and hearts while we go about our days completely oblivious. Thank you all for your service.

ABOUT THE AUTHOR

Kristine Allen lives in beautiful Central Texas with her adoring husband. They have four brilliant, wacky and wonderful children. She is surrounded by twenty six acres, where her five horses, five dogs and five cats run the place. Kristine realized her dream of becoming a contemporary romance author after years of reading books like they were going out of style and having her own stories running rampant through her head. She works as a night nurse, but in stolen moments, taps out ideas and storylines until they culminate in characters and plots that pull her readers in and keep them entranced for hours.

If you enjoyed this story, please consider leaving a review on the sales platform of your choice, to share your experience with other interested readers. Thank you! <3

Follow Kristine on:

Twitter @KAllenAuthor
Facebook: www.facebook.com/kristineallenauthor
Instagram: www.instagram.com/_jessica_is_kristine.allen_
BookBub: www.bookbub.com/authors/kristine-allen
Goodreads: www.goodreads.com/kristineallenauthor
All Author: www.kristineallen.allauthor.com/
Webpage: www.kristineallenauthor.com

Printed in Great Britain
by Amazon